S0-AWT-933

US $6.99 / CAN $7.50

ISBN 978-0-14-241141-4

9 780142 411414

50699>

EAN

bathroom
stuff

wash rug

math book
for Liz

put cat
out

Shower
and start
wash

pack
backpack—
application?

Out of
antibacterial
hand soap (get)

get more
soda

feed
moonpie

Spray stain
with bathroom
bleach

a novel

organize
a binder
for Liz

essay
essay
essay

buried

eat
breakfast

organize
morning
routine

work on
application

Change
living room
around

try a
throw rug

vacuum
everything

Clean car
and fill up

Stock up on
Post-its—seven
colors (bright)

dish soap
(get)

redo nail
polish

if Gordons
are still here,
sneak trash
into bin

give away
old clothes

pack
healthy
lunch

get the
mail

Be
spontaneous

give rug stains
another try with
dish soap and
a little bleach

get
dressed

brush
teeth

condition
hair

reorganize
fridge

Call Liz

ROBIN MERROW MacCREADY

"My mom's gone."

Liz grabbed my arm. "Gone? What are you talking about?"

I didn't know. *Why had I said that?* I didn't want to go over all the details of Mom and her screwups. Everyone knew her story, that she'd taken off before, but she'd been sober since spring. The longest time ever. I'd believed it was over.

"Did she take off with that guy again? What's his name, Dubwood or something?" Deb said.

The group laughed.

"That's what you call him, don't you, Claude?" she said.

"Oh, man, Claude. I can't believe she fell off the wagon again," Cindy said.

"Oh, no," Liz said. "I'm so sorry."

"That's how it goes. You knew it would happen," Matt said.

The floor blurred before me. I saw the broken bottles and I saw the crumbs. The silverware was in piles on the rug, and the spills, the stains, all of it, would be there forever. It was Mom's M.O. Make a mess and leave it—and leave me, for a while, at least. And when she came back, I'd have it all cleaned up for her, and then we'd act like nothing had ever happened.

Not this time. This time was different. I hadn't seen this one coming, and now I had a feeling of dread about it. There was a blackness to this that I couldn't identify.

So I lied.

OTHER BOOKS YOU MAY ENJOY

shop for
health food

mail letters
like you said
you would

change living
room around

make a
long-term
calendar

Dust/Polish
Day

spray stain
with bathroom
bleach

clean up
garden

pack
application
(it's due)

more cat
food (get)

buried

prepare for
hurricane

get books
from Liz
(just do it!)

clean coffee
pot and
do dishes

mail
letter from
yesterday

cupboards
(restock &
clean)

...shes

move into
Mom's room

...os for
...ringer??

vac around
litter box

wash wash
wash wash
wash

...ack
backback—
application?

note to self—
screw
spontaneity

...e a
...term
...dar

ROBIN MERROW
MACCREADY

clean clean
clean clean
...lean

out of
antibacterial
soap (get)

ask Ms.
Frost about
scholarship

return
bottles and
cans

...eview
saturday's &
sunday's lists

speak
An Imprint of Penguin Group (USA) Inc.

SPEAK
Published by the Penguin Group
Penguin Group (USA) Inc., 345 Hudson Street, New York, New York 10014, U.S.A.
Penguin Group (Canada), 90 Eglinton Avenue East, Suite 700, Toronto, Ontario, Canada M4P 2Y3
(a division of Pearson Penguin Canada Inc.)
Penguin Books Ltd, 80 Strand, London WC2R 0RL, England
Penguin Ireland, 25 St Stephen's Green, Dublin 2, Ireland (a division of Penguin Books Ltd)
Penguin Group (Australia), 250 Camberwell Road, Camberwell, Victoria 3124, Australia
(a division of Pearson Australia Group Pty Ltd)
Penguin Books India Pvt Ltd, 11 Community Centre, Panchsheel Park,
New Delhi - 110 017, India
Penguin Group (NZ), 67 Apollo Drive, Rosedale, North Shore 0632, New Zealand
(a division of Pearson New Zealand Ltd)
Penguin Books (South Africa) (Pty) Ltd, 24 Sturdee Avenue,
Rosebank, Johannesburg 2196, South Africa

Registered Offices: Penguin Books Ltd, 80 Strand, London WC2R 0RL, England

First published in the United States of America by Dutton Books,
a member of Penguin Group (USA) Inc., 2006
This Sleuth edition published by Speak, an imprint of Penguin Group (USA) Inc., 2008

3 5 7 9 10 8 6 4 2

Copyright © Robin Merrow MacCready, 2006
All rights reserved

CIP Data is available

Speak ISBN 978-0-14-241141-4

Printed in the United States of America

To Mum and Dad
Thanks for giving me spaces and places to dream.
Rob

. . .

••• ACKNOWLEDGMENTS •••

Thanks go to:

My sister Kate, who was there the night I began *Buried*. Sitting in Bookland of Brunswick, she said, "Oh my god!" That was all the encouragement I needed.

My critique group members: Patty Murray, Sandra Dutton, and Karen Allen. Also, Amanda Russell, who came and went but asked the hard questions. This group never lies and always works for the story. Thanks, friends!

My friend Debbi Michiko Florence, for listening to me grumble and being my e-mail buddy when the dream came true. Oceans won't keep us apart!

The Edgecomb Eddy School kids and teachers for encouraging me. And special thanks to Tanya Thibault, Terry Mulligan, and Joanne Krawic, who rescued me on more than one occasion. Your patience is endless . . . right?

Authors Alicia Erian, Lea Wait, Maria Testa, Elizabeth Searle, Carol Brightman, Jackie Manning, and Van Reid, who saw something in my words. I believed what you said.

Julia Burns Riley, Ph.D., M.S.W., who gave me the nod of approval that I needed. Thank you.

My editor, Julie Strauss-Gabel, who helped me to dig deeper than I thought possible. You are amazing!

Associate editor Sarah Shumway, who answered all my questions—some more than once. Thanks for holding my hand at the end.

Wendy Schmalz, special agent and guide, who steered me through the sometimes murky waters of the publishing world. You never laughed at my questions.

My husband, Pete, who supplied endless cups of tea and coffee, and put on the brakes when my fingers began to grow into the keyboard. You had faith in me when I needed it most.

My son Daniel, who kept my iTunes well stocked, and let me know when my memories of high school needed updating. You rock.

My son Forrest, who asked a lot of questions, the kind that helped me get unstuck. You could give Julie a run for her money in the future. You also make a mean sandwich.

buried

. . .

I float on angel wings over Mom's garden. I dip down to deadhead the flowers and toss them behind the workshop. A sound penetrates the mist, but I ignore it. I glide and dip and toss the flowers onto the mound. The pile grows until it's a small mountain of purples and golds. I have many more to add before I am done.

Though I'm not finished, I rest on an air current and look toward the beach. The moon has sunk behind the trees, and the sky over the sea is pink and purple, a hint that it is morning in Deep Cove. It's time to be done.

I reach out for the last bit of wind, tipping my wing like the birds do, and go back to work. With a blossom in each hand, I glide through the morning garden, but a sound pulls me down. Now I'm not floating, I'm falling, and I don't want to touch the ground. It's going to hurt. I tuck my feet under me and brace myself for a crash.

. . .

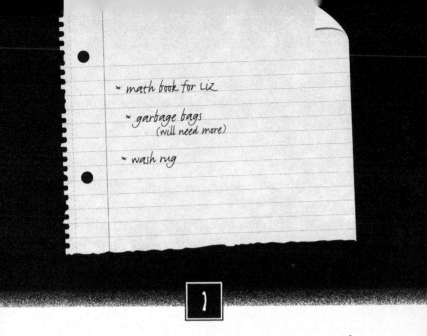

* math book for Liz

* garbage bags
  (will need more)

* wash rug

1

I JERKED AWAKE AND RAN TO THE PHONE in the kitchen, grabbing it before the machine could pick up. The sniffles on the other end gave away the caller immediately.

"What's wrong, Liz?" I asked, leaning on the counter. Relief washed over me. I could deal with Liz's problems.

"I—I can't do it," she said. "I just don't get it—I'll never get it." She let out a shaky breath and then sniffed. "Can you meet me at early study hall? Please, Claudine, please?"

"What time is it?" I asked, kicking aside an empty pizza box.

"Almost seven-fifteen." *Sniff.*

I looked around the room. Broken beer bottles, over-turned ashtrays, and snack foods littered the trailer from end to end. "I might be a little late. I haven't changed yet."

"Thank you, thank you. I love you, Claude!"

Shutting my eyes to the mess, I stepped carefully over a half-filled garbage bag. This was typical. Typical of Mom before she stopped drinking. She'd have a party and trash the place, then take off for a while. Last time it was South Carolina with Candy. *Later, I'll get to it later,* I thought.

Damn, here we go again.

I went to my bedroom, put on clean jeans, clipped up my long brown hair with a barrette, and slipped on my clogs. I made my bed and started a wash. At least my room was neat and organized.

Liz and I weren't the only ones at early study hall, but we found a table alone and sat side by side, the Algebra II book between us.

"Dad's going to kill me if I don't pass," she said. She swallowed a sob and pressed the heels of her hands to her eyes.

"Liz, you've got to get ahold of yourself. You can't do anything if you give in to every emotion. Especially this," I said, tapping her paper. "They're just numbers." I patted her back. "You do fine in everything else. You're even in a senior English elective with me this year, and you don't have trouble with that."

She shrugged. "This is math."

"You can do this."

She twirled her pencil between her fingers like she was bored with my pep talk.

"Take a cold, hard look at the problems and forget about your dad. Don't feel anything; just think."

"I hate this." She took a breath and looked at the page. "I don't even know what this means," she said. "Why are there letters *and* numbers? It doesn't make sense."

I explained the quadratic formula and made her a simple problem. She did it without a hitch. I gave her a harder one. She did that. Soon she had three more done, and they were all correct. "Now try the one on the paper."

"Too hard, Claude."

"Just try it," I said.

She bit her bottom lip. "Like the ones I just did, right?"

"Right."

She did it and then slapped her pencil down. "Done."

I leaned over her paper and nodded. "You did it."

"You're my guardian angel, Claude."

I thought of my dream. In it I was a falling angel, a crashing angel.

Could I pass as a guardian angel? Maybe.

Seniors were allowed one English elective a semester, and Semester One at Deep Cove High was poetry. Liz leaned toward me across the table we shared.

"Claudine," she said in a low voice.

My mind was a blank slate. No thoughts came, and for a panicky moment I forgot where I was. I looked up at Mr. Springer, and he nodded to me.

"It's your turn," he said.

My heart thumped in my chest. My turn? What was I supposed to be doing?

Liz pointed to the text, and I read each word separately and unrelated to the one before or the one after. When white space appeared, I stopped and looked up at him.

He raised his eyebrows. "Okay," he said. "For homework, come up with three Maine poets to share tomorrow. Class dismissed."

Liz was in my face immediately. "What was that? You sound like a zombie."

"Tired, I guess."

She looked at my hands. "Helping in your mom's garden?"

"What?" I looked at my black crescent nails. "Yup." I picked at them as we headed down the hall toward the double doors.

"Need a ride to group?" Liz asked. We backed up to the lockers as a clutch of noisy girls passed us. "I did that letter-writing exercise last night," she said.

"That was stupid," I said. "If you can't tell the truth face to face, why do it on paper and then throw it away?" Lydia, the facilitator of our group, Teens of Alcoholics, suggested writing our feelings to our alcoholic parent and then throwing the letter away. She thought it would help.

We stepped out into the sunlight, and I set down my backpack to fish out my sunglasses. "I didn't do it. And I think I'm getting sick of that group."

"Claude, you're the one who got me to go in the first place."

"I'm just not sure I need it anymore." I started down the granite steps ahead of her.

"You're lucky," she said.

I looked back at her suddenly. "Lucky?"

"You're so over it now. Just last week you were calling your mother twice a day. I need some of whatever you've got."

"It's just experience, I guess."

"Will you come anyway? I don't want to go alone."

The group met daily at the Community Center near the church, but wasn't affiliated with any group or any religion. It only offered the promise of anonymity and support. Liz and I went every other day when we could. I'd been going off and on for the last year. Knowing other people had the same problem always helped. But today I felt itchy and claustrophobic.

Every time I came into the high-ceilinged room, a wave of memories hit me and I felt like I was four again—pants dirty, my hair a tangled mess, my nose red and crusty. I went to preschool here. The Blue Bus picked me up and dropped me off every day.

I remembered the long tables and the tiny wooden chairs splattered with paint. This was where I learned how wonderful peanut butter was on graham crackers. This was where I loved to play house and make art. Every morning before snack we gathered in a circle on our mats and had Show-and-Tell. During Choice Time I climbed onstage and ran through the red velvet curtain over and over again just so it would caress my face. Sometimes I just wrapped myself in it and hid.

Now ten metal chairs scraped across the floor as the group gathered in a circle. I sat beside Liz, and Hanna sat beside me. I knew Hanna from school, but we never hung out together. She was captain of the cheerleading team. The clipboards came my way, and I took one. There were two pieces of paper on them: the steps to recovery and the beliefs.

Lydia, our facilitator, held a paper coffee cup and waited for the clipboards to make the rounds. She seemed a little nervous and nitpicky today, nodding as each person took one, like she had someplace to be. As soon as the last person got one, she tucked her red hair behind her ears and sat up straight. "My name's Lydia, and I'm an adult child of an alcoholic."

"Hi, Lydia," the group said.

I jumped. We did this every time, but it snuck up on me today. I alternately clung to my clipboard and picked at my cuticles, hoping for relief.

"As I've told you before, I'm just here as a facilitator. I'll only join in if you need me, or if I see a need." She looked at me expectantly. "Can you start us today, Claudine?"

I looked at Liz, then back at Lydia. "Okay. I'm Claudine. I'm a child of an alcoholic." My chair creaked. I sighed.

"Hi, Claudine," the group said.

I lined up my papers so the edges matched perfectly.

"Let's go around the room." By the time the greetings

were done, I had to have one of the steps picked out to discuss or another focus for the meeting.

"My name's Liz, and I'm the daughter of an alcoholic."

"Hi, Liz," we said.

Feet shuffled as each member of the group introduced himself or herself.

Matt from English class was also there. He'd come two other times, but when he talked, it was only so he could disagree or scowl at what was being said. The only time he'd ever talked to me was at a junior high dance, and when I'd said I wouldn't dance with him, he'd punched me in the arm. He was much cuter now, and his long, dark curls fit his bored expression. Now I'd probably dance with him if he asked.

As each person was greeted, my stomach became tighter, and I picked away at my skin as I weighed my options. I could pass a clipboard and have everyone take turns reading a step from the paper, or we could share our experiences with the letter writing. What could I say? I hadn't done a letter. Three more people. Three more people to go. No, two.

Now Chris wanted to talk about her letter to her mother that she'd torn up. This was supposed to be greetings, not share, but it worked for me. I sat back and crossed my arms.

"Why'd you tear it up?" Matt asked.

Chris shot him a dirty look. "Because I'm not cruel like you. I wrote it for myself, not my mother."

"You're just chickenshit," he said.

"And you're mean when you don't need to be."

I tried to imagine the letter I would've written if I'd done the exercise. My breath caught in my throat. It was almost my turn to speak. One more. Hanna piggybacked on Chris's comment about how freeing the letter writing was for her.

"But I gave it to my mom," she said, looking proud.

The group gasped in unison.

"Are you crazy?" Chris said.

Liz covered her mouth.

"It wasn't bad, really. I just expressed my feelings and told her it hurt me when she drank." Hanna looked at the floor. "She cried."

The room grew silent. This wasn't the cheerleader I knew.

Then all eyes were on me. A chair squeaked on the other side of the circle. My mind went to the scene I'd left at home that morning. I shared the only story I could.

"My mom's gone."

Liz grabbed my arm. "Gone? What are you talking about?"

I didn't know. *Why had I said that?* I didn't want to go over all the details of Mom and her screwups. Everyone knew her story, that she'd taken off before, but she'd been sober since spring. The longest time ever. I'd believed it was over.

"Did she take off with that guy again? What's his name, Dubwood or something?" Deb said.

The group laughed.

"That's what you call him, don't you, Claude?" she said.

"Oh, man, Claude. I can't believe she fell off the wagon again," Cindy said.

"Oh, no," Liz said. "I'm so sorry."

"That's how it goes. You knew it would happen," Matt said.

The floor blurred before me. I saw the broken bottles and I saw the crumbs. The silverware was in piles on the rug, and the spills, the stains, all of it, would be there forever. It was Mom's M.O. Make a mess and leave it—and leave me, for a while, at least. And when she came back, I'd have it all cleaned up for her, and then we'd act like nothing had ever happened.

Not this time. This time was different. I hadn't seen this one coming, and now I had a feeling of dread about it. There was a blackness to this that I couldn't identify.

So I lied.

"No. She didn't take off. Mom's in rehab." I put my fingertips on my lips as if to put the words back in.

"Rehab? That's great, Claude!" Liz said, slapping my back.

"Thanks," I said.

Chris and Deb looked at each other.

"I know I said she was doing great. She was, too, but she had a relapse. This time, instead of trying to do it on her own again, she decided to go for professional help." A few thumbs went up, a couple of smiles. I drank them in.

"So was it a fight?" Matt asked.

I fiddled with my clipboard while my face flushed. "No. Not at all."

"You're lucky," he said. "Getting my dad to do anything like that would take me and my brother a few hours. We'd probably have to carry him there."

It was the second time that day I'd been told I was lucky. I liked the idea of Mom in rehab, in the process of recovering. "In process" sounded like recovery was some sort of art or something. It was definitely better than running off with her boyfriend, Linwood, who was no prize, or with her friend Candy.

I leaned forward and rested on my elbows. "She was in process many times and always relapsed. The difference this time was the talking. We really communicated about it this time, and I let her know how I felt. She really heard me. Not just listening, *hearing*." I touched my ear. "You know what I mean?"

There were murmurs and nods. Lydia took a sip of coffee and sat back in her chair. Willa, one of the nicest girls in school, smiled and nodded once.

I continued on. "I knew when I told her the truth about what she was doing to me that it would make a difference. It did. We cried and then we hugged. It was really pretty simple." I looked over at Matt and smiled.

Liz leaned toward me and whispered, "I can't believe you didn't tell me."

I shrugged. "It's been a little crazy, I guess."

"Okay, time," Lydia said, putting down her cup. "Think about doing more letters. Remember, throw them out, tear them up. Whatever. You don't have to share them unless you think it's the right thing to do."

Liz dropped me off, and I walked across Sea Road, where the big summer cottages lined up side by side and faced the ocean. I took the path between the Smiths and the Gordons and crossed Beach Road. We lived on the corner of Sea Spray Acres. Our single-wide trailer and garage was the only property in the whole development, except for one new Cape way back on the cul-de-sac. When I was little and the bus picked me up on the corner, they called it Stinky Acres instead of Sea Spray Acres. I didn't figure out right away that it was me they were talking about. Once I did, I waited for the bus on the seawall, hoping the wind would blow away the stink.

Mom got offers on our place all summer long. A full acre of land was hard to come by so close to the ocean. She liked to pretend she'd sell it, but the place wasn't hers to sell; it belonged to my grandmother who lived in Florida. She threatened, off and on, to move back and build a rental. She wasn't happy about the deck Linwood had built over the roof of the garage, or the unruly garden Mom had created. "The place is an eyesore," she said.

Moonpie, our double-pawed cat, had been watching from the deck, and as I approached he padded down the stairs to me. He rubbed against my leg, but I ignored him and steadied myself for what I knew I'd see next.

I yanked the rattling storm door open and stepped into the trailer. At the sight of the room, I began to sweat, my heart rising with each beat. *Nobody can see this mess; nobody can know.* I whirled around and locked the door. *Breathe,* I told myself. *This is a disaster, but you know how to deal with it. It's your specialty, Claudine.* I navigated the trash and peeked into Mom's room. It was exactly as I'd left it. It was true, she was gone for sure. But why did she always do this to me?

I waded back through the mess and got the rubber gloves from the kitchen sink. I grabbed the garbage bag I'd started with the night before and began with the biggest chunks of brown glass. *One thing at a time,* I thought. *Just pick up the glass first.* I listened to the *clink-clink* as I tossed them into the trash bag. In an attempt to go faster, I gathered too big of a handful, and glass shards poked through the gloves, piercing my already raw skin. But I continued the job, double bagging the broken bottles and setting them aside. I started a different bag for the ashtrays, food wrappers, and general garbage. Any items that looked even remotely like trash were thrown in with the rest of the garbage. Old calendars, posters of places far away, half-melted candles. Anything that looked used, I tossed.

I vacuumed using all the attachments. I did the floors, the walls, the ceiling, the rugs, and the furniture. I lifted the window shades and sucked up the flies buzzing against the warm glass. Even the quickest ones were no match for me. It felt so good to be getting the place back to normal.

I vacuumed the foldout couch, the cushions, and the

beds. Then I stuffed the sour-smelling sheets in the washer and cranked the knob to HOT. I held my stinging hands under the water while the machine filled. I washed load after load while I scrubbed the bathroom and kitchen. And then there was the stain by the door.

The tan wall-to-wall carpeting was from the '70s, and I didn't have much hope of getting the stain out, but I had to try. I attacked it with a nailbrush from the bathroom and poured on stain lifter in a steady stream, but it only spread. It faded slightly but got bigger. Next I used rug cleaner that foamed. Even as I scrubbed the stain into a pink froth, I knew it would be there forever.

Under the kitchen sink was a half-empty bottle of pine-scented cleaner. I cleared the sink of soggy pizza crusts and poured it in. While the hot water foamed up billowy and high, I let the water soothe my burning skin. I held my hands out, my skin a deep pink against the white enamel sink, and inhaled the strong pine smell. It comforted me as I stared into the bubbles. I thought about how Mom hated to clean and how she knew I couldn't stand things dirty. It made me feel nervous when the trailer got cluttered, so I'd clean it for her and she'd let me.

I turned off the tap and squeezed out a sponge in the soapy water. Starting with the walls, I wiped off the sticky beer. With a swipe down the dark paneling, the streaks were gone. It seemed a waste to clean only the walls, so I did the trim in the kitchen and the living room. I'd never washed the wood, and I was sure Mom had never done it either. With every wipe, I washed away a party or a boyfriend who smoked or a bad day. With every swipe, a little of the past was gone and my future materialized. I had a fresh start, a clean slate, a new beginning.

I stood on the counter and straddled the stove. The first sweep over the top of the cupboards brought a rain of black jelly beans clattering to the floor. Like a flashback in a movie, it was suddenly sophomore year, a time when Mom was handling her drinking. It wasn't abstinence, but she was managing well. With her new outlook, she decided to do Easter, but by the time she got her act together, all the jelly beans in the stores were gone, except for the black ones. When I woke up that Sunday morning, I played little girl for her and found most of the beans, but it got a little creepy with Mom acting like I was precious all of a sudden. I ate some to keep her happy, so she'd stay in a good mood, but when she wasn't looking I threw them out with the rest of the garbage. In the end it didn't matter—she got drunk that afternoon anyway, and soon things were back to the way they'd always been.

I jumped down and sucked up the dusty black beans with the vacuum.

When I was through with the woodwork, greasy dust floated on top of the black water. I wondered how many years of cooking, of partying, of screaming at each other it represented. I rinsed out the sponge and pulled the plug.

As the sky darkened, I took the blankets and sheets outside, shook off the cigarette smoke, the beer, the memories, the mess, and one by one, hung them over the line to be blown clean by the September sea breeze.

Now it was my turn to get clean.

I ran the water hot and steamy. I covered a shower puff with citrus body wash and lathered myself from head to toe, letting the dirty water run down my arms and legs. I took the nailbrush and scrubbed my toes clean, carefully picking out the dark grime with my fingernails. All of the day's dirty mess pooled at my feet in a soapy mud puddle and swirled down the drain.

When I came out of the bathroom, fresh and clean, my eyes were drawn again to the stain in front of the door. It didn't look much better. Maybe it had spread more. It was darker, not just wetter. The rug cleaner directions said I could vacuum it up in two hours. I'd have to wait to see.

I went to Mom's room. A crisp, clean sheet covered her king-size bed, and only Moonpie lay curled in the center of it. I'd taken care of everything.

Being alone would be okay. I could do this. I'd done it before. Yeah, Mom was gone, but I should be okay with that, right? I lay next to Moonpie and dialed Liz's number. When she answered, I couldn't stop myself. I had to say it out loud again.

"Mom's gone." And again my hand went up to my mouth as if to stop the words, but they had come on their own.

"Claude?"

"Yeah," I said. "Mom's gone."

"I know. You told us, remember? So, is it a twenty-eight-day thing?"

"I don't know."

"Are you okay?"

I looked out to the living room. It was neat and tidy. No cigarette smoke hung in the air, and the only sounds came from my breathing and Moonpie's purr. "I'm fine. I just miss her even though she does stupid things sometimes." I held my thumb and forefinger to the bridge of my nose and squeezed, trying to hold back the tears. I imagined the group where Liz and I had been that afternoon and pictured Mom sitting there instead of driving down Route One in Linwood's pickup truck to god-knows-where.

"I still can't believe you didn't call and tell me," Liz said.

"Yeah, sorry. I was just surprised. I couldn't believe she started up again." I got up and opened Mom's closet. Empty, except for her winter coat. I turned away from the dark space. "But we had a big talk, and she decided to go get help. She's totally committed to getting sober this time."

My mother had been the main character of the most notorious drinking stories in Deep Cove, Maine. Now I had cast her in a rehab program, and she was getting sober. Even as I lied to Liz, I smiled to myself and let it sink in: Mom getting help, sharing her story, recovering. Finally.

"Wow, Claude," Liz said. "You've been waiting for this day. But did you tell us everything at group?"

I let my mind go blank until Liz asked, "Did you have another fight?" She sounded worried.

"No," I said too fast, shaking my head. "No fight. It wasn't like that at all," I said, looking at the garbage bags near the door. "She just finally hit bottom. Rock bottom.

After a rough night of drinking, she sat me down and said, 'Honey, I'm sorry for all I've put you through, and I'm finally going to do it. I'm going to get help.'"

"Perfect. That's how it's supposed to happen. I want Dad to apologize for being an ass and go to rehab like your mom."

"Hey, Liz, maybe you should do another one of those letters," I said.

"Yeah. You, too. You must have a lot you want to say to your mom."

Later, at the kitchen table, I stared at my homework. The words on the page meant nothing. This wasn't my usual routine. Most of my studying took place in the nooks and crannies of the day, usually in my room on top of my bed, buried in books. But for once, the trailer was quiet and clean. For once, I could study at home without a party going on around me, without a blaring TV or music pushing under the crack of my door.

The fridge buzzed behind me and the baseboard ticked, creating an annoying duet. The kitchen chairs creaked with every shift, with every breath. But above all that, a drone sounded. I stood up and closed my eyes to listen better. It turned off and then on again. I followed it to the open broom closet opposite the table and put my head through the door. Nothing at first, but then a loud, insistent buzz. Scooching down, I put my hand on the vacuum canister. The vibration was the unmistakable sound of angry flies, flies that were pissed off and wanted out. I closed the door, gathered up my homework, and cranked the stereo up. In my bedroom, I sat cross-legged and took my notes out again. The music seeped under the shut door. Now I could study.

It was late when heavy footsteps vibrated through the trailer.

"Serena!"

My mouth went dry.

"Serena, baby." I heard a six-pack clank on the counter, and my heart pounded against my chest. It was Linwood Dodge. *Without Mom*.

I kept still, not breathing, trying to think why he wasn't with Mom barreling down Route One, headed for nowhere.

He pounded past my bedroom, then came back and opened my door. "Where's your mother?" he asked, too loudly, as usual. His silhouette in the doorway made him appear larger than he was. "She around?"

I stared at him while the realization grew inside me. Mom really and truly wasn't with him. Linwood was here looking for her. Alone.

"Where is she, Claude?"

I shrugged. What could I say? She was supposed to be with him.

He threw up his arms and let them fall. "She finally leave me for that trucker guy?" He leaned against the door frame and crossed his arms, and then his ankles. Linwood was short, but he made up for it by lifting weights. His crater-scarred face made him hard to look at. "What's-his-name? Gary or somethin'?"

It was possible. *Of course.* Gary the trucker was one of her crushes. I nodded, mostly in approval of Mom's choice. If she had to choose between Linwood and Gary, Gary was the lesser of the two evils. I was about to say more, but the image of Mom sitting in a group circle appeared in my mind. I opened my mouth, then closed it.

"Spit it out, girl." He stepped into the room, and the familiar scent of fish bait mingled with my scented candle.

"Mom's gone to dry out. Maybe she'll be back and maybe she won't." I kept my eyes on my open book.

"One a them twenty-eight-day things?"

"Yeah, that's it," I said, turning an unread page.

He disappeared down the hall and then came back in. "She couldn't have planned it too well. She left her toothbrush." He held it up for me to see. Then he blew a smoky breath into my room. "One down, twenty-seven to go."

"Whatever." I kept my eyes on the page.

"Well, I doubt it'll work on your mother—she's a die-hard. You sure she didn't leave me for that trucker guy?"

Of course she had, I was sure now, but I couldn't say it—he'd flip out on me. "She's at rehab. I told you."

"You gonna see her?" He stepped closer.

"Nope, but when I write her, I'll tell her you came by, okay?"

As soon as I heard the door slam, I sprayed my room with air freshener.

I didn't blame her for leaving Linwood for clean-cut Gary. She and Linwood had a crazy on-off thing.

But why'd she leave me?

I flipped to the pink Post-it flag in my binder that said *Extra Paper*. I closed my eyes and saw Mom and Gary at a truck stop eating burgers and laughing. Gary was a better choice. But I made it fade away. I made it dissolve like in the movies, and I replaced the image with Mom in rehab chatting with a counselor, sharing sad stories and worrying about how much she might have hurt me. I saw Mom getting the cure before it was too late. But that picture dissolved back to Gary helping her into his tractor-trailer. She'd taken off and left me again.

Mom,

How is it that you think it's okay to just take off whenever you want? Man, that's unbelievable!!!! I would never do that to anyone. NEVER. If I did, I'd be just like you.

So you're with Gary. Is he better than Linwood? Probably. Is it better than living here with me? Probably. And Linwood wants me to tell you he came by. You're his one-stop shopping, I guess. Free food, free beer, free love. He's pissed. That's what you get for messing it all up again. You can deal with it when you get back, if you decide to come back.

—Claude

* try a throw rug

* try nailbrush

* if the Gordons are still here, sneak trash into bin

* give stain another try

* call Liz

2

OR THE SECOND DAY IN A ROW there was nobody to take care of but me. The trailer still smelled fresh and looked neat. I took the heart-shaped throw rug from my bedroom and covered up the stain near the door. It wasn't the best look, but it served its purpose.

It was trash day for the Gordons, so I snuck some garbage bags into their bin and walked to the beach to wait for the bus. The water was still and sparkly. Linwood would be out hauling traps on a day like this. In the distance, a diesel engine growled as it moved from pot to pot, and I squinted to see whose it was. It wasn't the *Serena*. *Too bad he is such a dub*, I thought. *Mom might have married him.*

I kicked off my clogs and jumped into the sand. This was our beach spot—right across from the path to Sea Spray Acres. I thought about Flower Child, Mom's summer business, and how it began right here on my last day of second grade. We'd been having a picnic, and I was wearing shorts and begging Mom to let me go swimming. Mom had on a floppy straw hat she'd decorated with dried flowers and shells, and Candy and Sylvia were teasing her about it. A lady walked by with her tiny brown dog. She'd gone by our towel once, but on her way back she came over.

"Where'd you get your hat?"

"This?" Mom said, putting her hand on her head. "I made it."

"I'm going to a luncheon and would love to show up with a hat like that." Her dog was running circles around her, so I held out a crust to him. He gobbled it up and begged for more with two paws. "Could I pay you to make one for me?"

Mom says that Candy and Sylvia laughed after the lady had left, but I don't remember that. I just remember the way Mom's face lit up, surprised like a kid.

Mom had a business going with the luncheon ladies by the end of that summer, and in the fall she turned the garage into her workshop. The next summer she had a cart decorated with dried flowers that said FLOWER CHILD'S BASKETS AND BOUQUETS. She hung hats from the awning and piled the top shelf with baskets. We'd walk the sidewalk from our beach spot down to Seaside Cottages, then past Big Beach, Mother's Beach, and all the way down to Deep Cove. Then we'd do it again. It wasn't so bad. We'd stop to see all her friends, and when the weather kept the tourists home, we'd go home, too. She was happy in the summertime. Gardening, walking, making things.

I hopped back up on the wall and put on my clogs. I didn't want to think about it, but the truth was that when fall came, and the clocks were turned back, I knew she'd turn, too. She stopped making things and went into a kind of angry hibernation until spring.

The squeak of the bus doors brought me back, and I got on and settled into a seat. The bus took us by Seaside Cottages, where Mom worked with Candy sometimes, past Deep Cove Downs, the MacPhees' road, and then by the rocks where Mom and I scavenged for shells, beach glass, and driftwood for her wreaths and baskets.

In English, I was still thinking about Mom and scribbling on my paper when Mr. Springer called on me, with only five minutes left of class.

"I—I—"

Muffled laughter came from behind me. What was I supposed to be doing?

"Are you with us?" he said. He pushed his glasses up on his long, bony nose.

I shrugged.

"Maine poets?"

"Edna St. Vincent Millay," I said.

"Good. Let's hear something."

I looked at my paper, where I'd doodled a flower wreath around the word REHAB. I covered it with my hand and closed my eyes. My throat tightened.

Liz whispered, "Read the poem you brought."

I fumbled through my notebook. I hadn't brought a poem.

Mr. Springer shook his head and turned to someone else.

I looked down at my hands, red and dry from scrubbing the trailer the day before. I picked at a smudge of lead on my pointer finger. If the intercom hadn't clicked on, I might have made a hole in my skin.

"Claudine Carbonneau, please come to the office."

I looked up at Mr. Springer. He gave a stiff nod. "Might as well take your books."

"Meet me at lunch," Liz said.

All eyes were on me as I walked to the back of the classroom and slipped out the door. I breathed slowly, forcing my heart to stop its pounding. There was no reason to feel panicked, I told myself, it's probably nothing. But I kept thinking of Mom.

The empty halls echoed with my footsteps as I walked alone past classes in session. I tried to think about how much I loved school, how much I loved walking into the old brick building every day and looking up into its airy ceilings.

I breathed in the school smell: cleaning fluid and wax polish. Most people hated school and saw it as a prison, even Liz. What I hated was the interruption of snow days, holidays, and teacher workshops. I was always the one with the pissy look on my face when a false alarm sent us home.

Again, thoughts of Mom crept into my mind, and I pushed them down deeper. I focused on the most immediate things: the scuff of my clogs down the hall, the slam of a classroom door, the cool silkiness of the banisters. I looked into each classroom window as I went past and made myself focus on the faces. I changed my mind from panic to peace.

When I saw Ms. Frost, the guidance counselor, in the office, I blurted out, "Is it my mother?"

"No, no, Claudine," she said. Taking some papers from an envelope, she said, "I just wanted to have a word with you about the Charles Hart Scholarship. The one I talked about last week."

I stared at the pages as she flipped through them. Ms. Frost had talked about this scholarship at the senior assembly the week before. It was for people who had the grades but not the money. My mouth went dry, and my mind raced. I'd been hoping for it.

Ms. Frost took a pencil out of her halo of silver braids and smiled, her light blue eyes crinkling at the corners. "You know how I feel about you, Claudine. You're very bright and capable, and you have a chance to be whatever you want to be. I want to help you get there." She sighed, then smiled, drawing out the moment. "I'm nominating you," she said.

I flung my arms around her. "Thank you, thank you, thank you. You won't be disappointed."

"Of course I won't. It was an easy decision. Not a home run yet, but I have faith in you."

She wrote the due date on the envelope.

"Just take it home and look it over. It's a full scholarship to the state university. Your mother needs to fill out the financial aid information," she said. "It's crucial—"

"Mom's gone to rehab."

"Oh," she said, sounding surprised. "That's good, isn't it?"

I nodded. "She'll call and I'll tell her about this." I reached for the papers, but she tucked them in the envelope.

"She'll call? Where is she?"

I didn't miss a beat. "Jackson Heights." I watched as Ms. Frost took it in.

"Oh, Jackson Heights, the one in Portland."

I nodded, feeling the sweat prickle in my armpits.

"Well, that facility has a very good reputation. She'll have the best care there." She handed the envelope to me. "When she calls, get the information, and we'll look it over together before we put it in the mail. It has to be postmarked two weeks from today, or you'll miss the deadline."

"No problem," I said. I zipped it in my backpack. "Thanks, Ms. Frost."

"No thanks necessary. You deserve it, Claudine."

I thought about Jackson Heights as I walked to my next class. It was one of the best facilities in New England. I'd bargained and even begged Mom to call about the programs, and now I imagined her there, sitting in a group circle, being open and honest. I saw her listening to the hard truth and feeling the pain, being called on her shit.

At noon I made a beeline for the corner table, my regular seat, and dropped my lunch bag. I went to the pay phone and tucked the receiver into the crook of my neck and dropped in a quarter. Liz appeared at my side, a diet soda in each hand.

"Claude, what are you doing?" Some fizz bubbled down the side, and she slurped it up before it reached her hand.

Annoyed at her sloppiness, I turned my back and pressed the receiver to my ear.

"Remember, you don't have to call her anymore," she said. She took a sip and went to her seat.

I listened to the purr of the dial tone and to the crinkle of Liz's cellophane, probably a Little Debbie cake. I'd forgotten. *Mom's gone.* I counted the metal ridges of the phone cord: *One, two, three, four . . .*

"Claudine, she's not home. Remember?"

Now I had to start over: *One, two, three, four, five. One, two, three, four, five. One, two, three, four, five.* There. I felt calm and hung up the phone.

"I was just calling Jackson Heights," I said.

She nodded and took a bite of her cake. "Jackson Heights? Wow. So, how's your mom doing?"

"Great, I guess. The message said they were on a lunch break."

She offered me some corn chips. I shook my head.

"I haven't touched them yet. Really, Claude."

I took some and sat down across from her.

"You gonna call later?" she said, her mouth now full of chips.

"Of course."

Calling to check on Mom was a daily chore. Sometimes things were fine, but sometimes I had to run home. It started in second grade when I was in the nurse's office sick with a fever. Nurse Gooch called Mom to come get me. I lay on the cot behind the screen listening to the squeak, squeak of her rubber soles until sleep pulled me down. Over and over I woke with sudden chills, only to fall into a sweaty sleep again. When Mom finally came, I knew it wasn't a dream, because I could hear voices behind the screen. Nurse Gooch said something like, "fever of one hundred and four . . ." and, "I've been meaning to talk with you about your daughter's hygiene . . ." I tried to open my eyes, but I couldn't stay awake. Mom raised her voice and said, "I don't think so. You have no clue about my life. You have no right to butt into it."

"All I'm saying is that we're concerned. Everyone is. And her teacher says that the other kids are noticing."

Mom helped me up, and we walked down the hall. The next thing I knew I was home in bed and feeling better. The TV was on in the living room, and I could hear the music from a soap opera. There was a bowl of soup on the floor beside my bed with a wrinkle of yellow fat over the top of it.

I lay back on my pillow, my head throbbing, and looked at my snow globe on the bedside table. It had been a birthday gift from Mom, and I'd always kept it by my bed. I reached over and jiggled it a little, watching the snow swirl in slow motion and cover the bright green grass. The yellow-haired princess remained still. Nothing fazed her. I had created armies to attack her, and she'd fended them off without a hitch. She'd even been taken from her castle, but she'd escaped and come back just in time to rescue the queen. Today the princess was tired and needed to rest for her next battle.

I woke later in the dark.

"Mom," I called. Her shadow rose on the living room wall against flashes of TV light.

"Better?" she said, lying down beside me.

I felt the covers tighten around me as she moved close. "I hate getting sick," I said. "I missed art, didn't I?"

"Yeah, art and whatever you have on Fridays."

"Today's Friday?" I lifted my head and felt my skull bones bang together.

"Yup." Mom brushed my hair back from my eyes. "You were some sick, Angel."

I snuggled into her arms and closed my eyes again. "Why doesn't Nurse Gooch like my high jeans?"

Mom gave me a squeeze. "Don't listen to what Nurse Gooch says. It's none of her business." She kissed the top of my head. "And it's *hygiene*, not *high jeans*. Besides, you don't smell. You'd tell me if someone teased you, right?"

I nodded, but my stomach tightened at the thought of her calling school. She'd made a scene at the Open House earlier in the year when she thought Miss White had given me free lunch. Mom wouldn't listen when Miss White told her she had nothing to do with the lunch program. I didn't like the look on my teacher's face when Mom raised her voice. She looked scared and embarrassed at the same time, and she kept playing with her bracelets.

I rubbed my belly to get the tightness out.

"How many times I wash your clothes or give you a bath is none of that nurse's business." She leaned over and gave me a kiss—cigarettes and beer.

I pulled away from her and touched my feet to the floor. "I have to pee." I held my throbbing head as I walked through the living room. Empty brown bottles littered the coffee table. I lined them up in a straight row and counted them, touching the open mouth of each one: one, two, three, four, five. When I came out, she was back on the couch, peeling off a label and crying. I counted. Still just five.

"Don't be sad, Mom." I sat beside her and wiped a tear from her cheek. "What's wrong?"

She covered her face. "I can't do this anymore. I just can't."

I twisted her long, dark hair and laid it down the center of her back.

"It's so hard. I can't do this alone."

"Do what alone, Mom?"

"Be a mother. Be me," she said, peeling the corner of her beer label.

"It's okay, Mom. I'll be your helper. I'll always be your helper."

A few days later, I found a couple of Nurse Gooch's pamphlets that Mom had thrown in the trash: GOOD HEALTH AND HYGIENE HABITS FOR GIRLS and MAKING GOOD HEALTH A HABIT. They had cute pictures of gleaming toothbrushes and sparkling bars of soap on the covers. One had a mother in an apron and pointy shoes, and the other had a checklist on a clipboard. The list had checks beside things like *brush teeth, wash hands, take a bath*. I took them out of the trash and read them over and over until I could recite them myself. I began lists just like the mother in the pamphlet. Soon my lists were tailored to my life: *make bed, wash dishes, check on Mom, make dinner.*

Now I really was her helper.

Part of me heard Liz calling my name, but the other part wanted to stay with Mom.

"Claude!"

Liz's voice brought me back to the cafeteria; the sounds of silverware being tossed and plastic trays being stacked kept me there.

"Where were you?"

"Just thinking." I wiped my apple and took a bite of it, then I smoothed the wrinkles from my bag.

"About?" she said.

"Nothing."

"Something, I know."

I shrugged.

I polished another spot on my apple and bit in. "Okay, I'm thinking that I'm alone at last." I took another bite, though I hadn't finished chewing the first.

"Claudine, are you telling me everything?" Liz leaned toward me and raised her eyebrows.

"Here's the truth," I said.

"Yeah . . ." she said.

"Mom and I did have a blowup before she left for rehab." I went to the trash and dropped my unfinished apple in the bucket.

When I came back, she said, "What about?"

I threw up my arms like it was obvious. "The usual," I said, sitting again. "It wasn't so bad, really. I had my say, she had hers, and we both agreed that rehab was the best place for her," I said.

"I can't believe you didn't call and tell me after," she said.

We'd always told each other everything, even though we were an unlikely pair. I had saved her butt in second grade when she couldn't regroup her addition problems, and she and her mom had taken me to Girl Scouts because my mother was not a normal mother.

"I guess I was just busy. You know, packing for her stay. Getting her ready." The story came fast and sure. Liz and I understood each other. I could talk to her about anything, but something kept me locked up about Mom.

Liz frowned. "Mmm."

The warning bell rang, and Liz stuffed the rest of her lunch into her insulated bag. "I'm freaking out about that health report I have to write. Will you help me, Claude? Please?"

"Don't I always?" I wrote, *Call Liz about report* and

Pick up floor cleaner and vacuum bags on the back of my lunch bag.

Liz peered over the table at what I was writing. I covered it with my hand.

"I can't believe you're making a list of cleaning chores. *Vacuum bags?* Oh my god, Claude. I love you, but you're such a geek."

I folded the bag into a square and put it in my pocket. "Don't worry—you're on the list."

She frowned at me. "You look kind of out of it. Are you okay?"

"I'm fine. Just a lot to do. How are you doing?"

"Good. Really good. It's the group. I'm glad you talked me into going. It's amazing, don't you think?"

"Amazing?" I stood up and wiped up our crumbs. Then we merged with the line leaving the cafeteria.

"The other day, when I was done sharing and it was so quiet, I thought I'd made a complete fool out of myself, but everyone was smiling and nodding. And I'm surprised by how many people we know from school." She leaned forward. "I mean, that cheerleader? And the agreement that it's all anonymous."

She said "anonymous" like it was a new word I'd never heard.

"I know the drill. I've got all the books, too."

When I got home from school, Moonpie came out from behind the workshop and met me at the steps, rubbing against my legs. I picked him up and felt him purr, smelling the earth on his paws.

"Where have you been?" I said, pushing my face into his long, tawny fur. He squirmed from my arms and shot back across the garden.

Inside, the answering machine was blinking. It was Liz's mother, the original owner of the machine; she'd insisted on giving it to us when she got her cell phone.

"Serena, it's Marty MacPhee. There's a Boosters meeting Thursday night, and we're hoping you'll make up some of your lovely fall baskets to sell at the fair. Call me."

Marty never gave up. I think she figured that Mom would improve herself with each hand-me-down or kindness. But Mom didn't get it; she just liked getting the next new thing. "Why does Marty keep giving us stuff?" she'd say. "She's already going straight to heaven. But don't tell her to stop though, okay?"

I made a note to take Mom's baskets to Mrs. MacPhee and pressed the next message. It was Candy, pissed off that Mom didn't show for work at Seaside Cottages.

I dialed her number. Then hung up. What would I tell her about Mom? Leaning against the kitchen counter, I fiddled with the stuff in the junk basket, pocketing some change. With a stab of pain, I thought about Mom leaving me. Not for a road trip with Candy, but for Gary.

I felt sick knowing it was so easy for her to walk away. I dialed again and counted the coins in my pocket: *One, two, three, four, five, one, two, three, four, five, one, two, three, four, five.*

"Where the hell is she?" Candy said. "She didn't show up for work, and I had to do all the checkouts alone. This weekend will be a big one, ya know, we're full." I heard her exhale on the other end of the line. "Well?"

I took out a pen and made lines on a pad of paper. I couldn't say it out loud. I couldn't say she'd left me for a guy. Again. "She's at a rehab program, Candy."

She laughed. "Rehab? Not Serena, she wouldn't go unless someone went with her. Linwood maybe? But I doubt it. Besides, she was wasted again the other night."

I dropped the pen and shoved the paper aside. "You knew about that? Why didn't you tell me?"

"Falling off the wagon was up to her. Besides, she and Gary were getting cozy again, and I didn't want to interfere with that. He was leaving in the morning."

"I could've stopped her if you'd just called me. I was just over at Liz's having dinner. Christ, Candy!" My stomach flipped over. "You could've called me. I would've stopped her."

"Jesus, Claudine. She's a big girl." She exhaled again.

I didn't want her to be with Gary. I wanted her in rehab, and I wanted to be the one who put her there. If I'd known—if I hadn't gone to Liz's house . . . "Well, she decided it was time to get serious. She's in rehab and won't be able to work for a while."

"I guess it's about time she got it under control."

"Yup. It's about time."

"Can you fill in when I need someone?"

"Just call me."

I hung up and went to Mom's room, dragging the vacuum behind me. I sat on the edge of the bed and looked around the room, trying to remember if I'd done the ceiling yet. A lone buzz came from the vacuum. He sounded pissed off, like he didn't like being alone. Under the shade, another fly threw himself against the window. Without leaving the bed, I pointed the wand at the fly and turned the vacuum on.

"Now you're not alone," I said.

Then I did the walls and ceiling while I stood in the middle of her bed. Even though the floor had been done, I did it again, this time reaching under the bed with the hose. A metallic clink went up the hose and into the vacuum. Fear ripped through me. My hand shook as I turned it off. I leaned the vacuum against the wall and shut the door.

I lined up five pages of the application form on the kitchen table, evening up the pages with the edge of the kitchen table. Then I began reading. The first page said I'd been nominated by Ms. Frost, a staff member of the high school. It said I qualified for a full scholarship to the state university, but I needed to fill in all the requested information and write a four-page essay.

Ms. Frost knew the problems I was dealing with. She'd witnessed one of Mom's binges firsthand at last year's Spring Banquet. I was a junior and had made High Honors in English, the only one with an A+ average.

Liz and her mother had noticed that Mom was drunk and offered to sit with her in the back of the room while I received the award. Even with several hundred people in the auditorium, her cries still reached me.

"My baby, my only baby. You're such an angel, my princess. Why are you so good to me, Claudine?"

The hum of disapproving voices grew in the audience until Ms. Frost finally took her out to the lobby. On the way out, I heard her go on and on.

"You have no idea how good Claudine is to me. She does everything." Even while the people in the audience clapped for me, they craned their necks to watch my mother as she was escorted out. As I sat on the stage, I tried to read the minds of the parents. What were they thinking? Was it pity? Disgust? They were probably shaking their heads in disbelief at how the same woman who made gorgeous dried-flower wreaths also made a drunken scene. *Well, she does live in a trailer*, someone might have said. *And you know, she doesn't have a husband.*

After that night, Mom made a deal with me to go on a health regime. All health food, exercise, and no alcohol. She was fabulous from last May to August.

I filled in the first line, printing carefully. APPLICANT: CLAUDINE MARIE CARBONNEAU.

The phone rang, jolting me from the task. It was Liz. "Have you started?"

"Started?"

"Springer's homework. The poet biographies. We're having a quiz on Thursday." I could hear her crunching on something. I looked at the clock. It was after six, and I hadn't eaten since lunch.

"Did I miss something?"

"No, it's on the assignment schedule." She rustled a paper. "The one that's due September twenty-first."

"I haven't done it." I had four pages to go on the application.

"I haven't either. I'll pick you up at the mailbox."

I touched each page, counting. One, two, three, four, five.

Deep Cove Library was open until nine. We only needed to find and photocopy some information.

Liz was on one end of the poetry stack, and I was at the other. "You're kind of out of it again. Maybe you should stay with us while your mom's gone."

"Don't tell your parents about Mom being at rehab."

"Too late, already did."

"Really?"

"Yup. I was worried about you. Mom looked to heaven and crossed herself and said something about praying for her."

"Sounds like your mom, but tell her no thanks."

I settled at a long table with two biographies. Liz thunked a pile of books down across from me. I looked at her, flipping through pages on Coatsworth.

"You know she means well," she said. Liz looked so together, effortlessly pretty, happy.

I couldn't help staring. *Liz, you have it all,* I thought.

"Did you say something?" she asked, tucking her straight blond hair behind her ear.

"I was just thinking how much I wish I was you."

"Even though my mother would drive you nuts." She crossed her eyes.

I stacked my books so the spines were even. "Even though." I peeled off all the colored Post-it flags from my dividers and arranged them in a row on the edge of the long table. "Things are just harder than they used to be," I said.

"What's up?" Liz said, leaning in.

I rehearsed the possibilities in my head: *Yeah, Mom took off again. She's with Gary. She fell off the wagon. Again. Left me to take care of myself, yet again. And she didn't clean up her mess, as usual. No, Liz, the rehab program was just wishful thinking.*

"Nothing's up," I said.

"Nothing except that your mom's at the top rehab program in the state."

I rearranged the Post-its from lightest to darkest. I almost had all the colors of the rainbow, but I needed a dark blue. I searched my binder pouches.

"Claudine, maybe I never told you, but I've always wanted your brains," she said.

I zipped up the binder without looking at her.

"You know that, Claude. Ever since second grade. And the help you gave me on that math assignment yesterday, that was exactly what I needed. And the help you'll be giving me on that health report . . . you'll help me, won't you? Look at me, Claude."

"Yeah," I said, tapping my head. "My brains, your looks. What a package."

"What are you saying, Claude? You're pretty. You just—"

"I need a bath, right?" I said, remembering Nurse Gooch and the teasing on the bus.

"Oh my god, are you a little PMS? I was about to say that confidence is all you need. You've kind of lost yours."

I nodded like I was considering it, but it was easy for her to say. Everything was in place for her. Even with only average SATs, she'd still be going to the college of her choice.

And now that I didn't have to deal with Mom at home, and with the application for the scholarship, maybe I'd be going, too.

At home, when I should've been working on my poet biography or the application, I wrote another letter, the kind I wanted to burn.

Dear Mom,

Okay, so if you decide to come back, there are going to be some changes. Here are the rules:

1. Say "Thank you" when you should, like when Mrs. MacPhee gives us something, or "No, thank you" if you don't want it. (You always joke or make a wiseass crack instead, and that's embarrassing. You aren't that funny, Mom.)

2. Be a clean drunk. Like Mr. MacPhee. Man, it's embarrassing when you're slouched over Linwood or Candy or slurring your words. Why do you do that???

3. Let me know when and where you're going. Make

a plan; don't just disappear. It's rude to take off without telling anyone.

You can start now. If you're out in some big rig with Gary the trucker, a call would be nice. It would be considerate. I actually worry when I don't hear from you. There's a dark something inside me, and it wakes me up at night and makes me scared for you, so call me, please.

—Claude

straighten up mess in garden

bring in flowers—make it nice

bake brownies for Liz

spritz room with air freshener

*call & remind Liz
to bring notes*

3

AT LUNCHTIME LIZ DROPPED HER LUNCH BAG beside me and said, "Are we on for after school?"

"Yeah, my place," I said, lining up my baby carrots evenly. *One, two, three, four, five.* I ate one.

"I'll bring what I started for health, and we can look at the notes for the poetry quiz."

"What quiz?"

"What quiz? The one tomorrow. It's prep for the test."

"Hmm." I touched each carrot, then ate one. Three left. "Liz, do you think it's bad to give someone a lot of chances?"

"What do you mean?"

"I don't know. What if you tried and tried to make it

work and just got so tired, you couldn't do it anymore?"
One, two, three, eat one, two left.

"Love changes things. Maybe your mom and Linwood need a break. And nobody makes good decisions when they're emotional."

I washed down the carrot with my spring water, but I really wanted Liz's Diet Coke.

"How'd you get so smart, Liz?" I said.

"I have smart friends. Also, Dad and I were talking last night. He's not so bad sometimes."

One, two, eat one, one left. I loved the last carrot. It was sweeter, tastier, special.

The warning bell rang, and Liz stood, grabbed her wrappers, and popped my carrot into her mouth.

I looked at the place where the carrot had been and then at her. Heat tingled under my cheeks.

"What?" she said, jaw grinding up and down. "Did you want that? It took you so long to eat them. Sorry. I figured you weren't so into them."

I couldn't speak. I waved her off and headed for the line out of the cafeteria.

"Claude, it was just a carrot." She leaned on me. "I'll buy you a new bag, an economy-size bag, a whole farm!" She squeezed me tightly.

I shook my head and looked up at the lights. "Don't worry about it," I said, picking the skin at my fingertips. But I couldn't stop thinking about it. She took the last one. My last carrot. I had to have more.

On the way to group, Liz stopped so I could get a bag of baby carrots.

"You, my friend, are a nut. You need to eat more puff pastry and less vegetables!" She opened a raspberry cream pie and offered me the first bite.

I shook my head. "You don't know where that's been, Liz."

She pulled onto the road. "It's been in a nice clean machine, Claude. Take a bite."

"No, thanks," I said. I held out a handful of carrots to her before she could stick her hand in the bag. "You never know who might have sneezed into the cream filling."

She held up her hand in stop sign fashion. "No, I've had my limit. And robots don't sneeze."

Liz started off the group by saying she wanted to hear what people thought about the letter-writing thing.

Stupid, I said to myself.

Matt said, "Why write it down and burn it or whatever? Why not just say it?" He kicked out his legs and crossed them.

I had to agree. It seemed like a wasted step, but then Mom wasn't around to talk about this stuff. And even if she were around, she wouldn't listen—not when she was drunk.

"I like it," Hanna said. "I need the space to think. On the paper, you know? It helped me to figure out that I'm not as upset with Dad as I thought."

Lydia was watching, but I couldn't tell how she felt. She was such a stone face. Blake was another one, but he always looked a little sad. But it could just be the extra folds of fat in his face.

"Well, I like it, too," Liz said. "I wrote a ton of letters and threw out each one. They started angry and didn't make any sense at all. Just a bunch of screams on paper, I guess." She laughed and a few others did, too. "Then I started talking to myself. It was so cool. I think I get what I'm upset about now." She sat back and grinned.

"So, what about you?" Matt asked.

Liz poked me with her elbow.

"What?"

"Matt asked you about your letters."

"Oh. Well, before Mom left for rehab, I forgot to tell her how proud I was that she was making such a big commitment. So I used the letter as a way to write it all down. Maybe I'll send it to her at Jackson Heights."

"Wow, Claude, you're lucky to have a parent who gets it," Deb said.

"Well, it's been a few years of back and forth. So I guess it's finally time. She's doing well. I heard from her last night. She left a message on the machine." I shifted in my seat and looked at the group.

"You didn't tell me that!" Liz said. "That's great!"

There were nods, and even Blake managed to curve the edges of his mouth into a grin. Everyone was smiling at me. Except for Matt.

After group we took the long way around the beach, around Deep Cove and Mother's Beach, with the windows rolled down and the music turned up, feeling the last bit of summer in the air. Already the wind had shifted, and we were getting hints of fall storms, but the lightness of the sky still said summertime.

"Last year was so easy," Liz said. She turned down the radio.

"Yeah," I said.

"What changed?"

"I don't know." I looked away.

"Claude, you've known my dad a long time. Why do you think he won't stop drinking?"

"Actually he doesn't drink that much, only till he reaches his Pleasure Zone, right?"

She downshifted and turned onto Beach Avenue. "He used to do that, but now it's more and more."

"You want to borrow that book with the exercises in it?"

"Maybe." She closed the window. "I guess."

"Remind me when we get inside."

"Maybe I just need to talk to him. Like you and your mom did."

An unexpected lump filled my throat, and I swallowed hard as we turned the corner of Sea Spray Acres, pulled over, and parked in front of the trailer.

"Thanks for helping me with this report. I'd be dead without you."

I stared out the windshield at the nose of Mom's white VW, parked like she'd never even left. My heart thudded, and for a second I thought she might be home.

"Claude?" Liz shook my shoulder. "Claude?"

"It's nothing." I got out of the car and walked to the steps.

Liz lagged behind, looking out at the garden. "Wow, I haven't been here since—"

"Forever?"

"Yeah, since that time—" she said.

"That time you came to pick me up for a sleepover and Mom was smashed out of her mind and tried to hug you and you freaked out and waited in your van with your freaked-out mother."

She laughed. "I was a little surprised, that's all." She stepped closer to the garden. "But wow," she said, looking around. "When did she do all this? She really pulled it together."

After that episode with the hugging, I'd banned Liz from the trailer and always had her pick me up at the sea-wall. I never invited anyone over when Mom was drinking. Just like Liz never invited anyone over unless her dad was in his Pleasure Zone.

The giant sunflowers nodded against the trailer, covering the rust. In front of them were hollyhocks, mallow, and a crawling yellow flower that filled in the empty spots. The individual beds of herbs, perennials, and annuals spread out from there, spilling over onto the paths that connected the beds to the workshop.

"She does okay in the summer," I said. "Better than before, anyway." I remembered the trailer during the bad times: shades down, filled with smoke, Mom's unwashed hair and rumpled clothes. A million years ago, it seemed.

But this time I walked up the steps and opened the trailer door without a trace of anxiety. "Come on in."

"Wow, this place looks incredible," she said. "What'd you do to it?"

"I cleaned it out. No big deal." I caught her staring at my red hands, and I put them in my pockets. "Put your stuff anywhere," I said.

Liz threw her coat and backpack on the couch and went to the kitchen. "Can I get a drink?" she asked.

I told her where the soda was and asked her to bring the brownies I'd made. I moved her things off the couch, hung her coat on a hook, and put her backpack out of the way of traffic. The slipcover had come out of the cracks of the couch and I straightened it out. When I turned around, Liz was staring at me.

"What?" I said.

"You're every mother's dream," she said.

We sat cross-legged on the floor and ate brownies and talked about guys and who was with whom this year. Every once in a while I got a jolt of panic and wondered if Mom was going to blow in with Linwood or Candy or Gary and settle in to party, but then I remembered that it was just me and I laughed a little louder, felt a little happier. It was like having my own apartment.

"While you're in this great mood, Claude, can you get me started?"

"Oh, yeah, no problem." I spread her notes out on the floor and took a look.

"I have to write a report for health about a current topic."

"You mean like cloning," I said.

"Like any current topic," she said. "But it has to be written"—she made quotation marks in the air—"through the lens of a scientist."

"It's obvious, Liz. You have the perfect subject at home."

She gave me a blank look. "Home?"

"Yeah, make it about alcoholism." I jumped up and ran to my room. I came back with all my books. "I don't need these anymore. You can cover the history of alcohol use, the beginnings of AA, current thoughts, health dangers. Everything."

She didn't look thrilled. "Maybe I'll make it about drunk driving. Maybe."

I got her another soda and opened up a book of affirmations. "Listen to this," I said. "'Denial is a river in Egypt.'" I laughed and slapped her knee. "That's where you are, in denial."

Liz was staring at the books like they were poison. She bit her bottom lip. "What are you talking about? I'm not in denial. I know my dad has a problem."

She had so much to learn. This would be a great project for her. "What do you think?" I asked.

She shrugged.

"Brainstorm first," I said.

She picked up her notebook and sighed dramatically. "Okay, shoot."

"Are you waiting for me to come up with the idea?" I shook my head.

"Yeah, just get things going for me. You always help me think."

"Okay. Statistics, family dynamics, and the science of it, like what it does to your body—exactly what it does!" I loved it. The ideas came from nowhere, one after another.

"This is great, Claude, really great. And we could make a big poster with a timeline of alcohol through the ages."

"And you can use all my books for your bibliography." I stacked them neatly so the titles showed: *The Elephant at the Table; Paddling Denial River; My Journey and Back.*

"Will you work with me on it tomorrow?" Liz said. "And after we can study for the English test."

"What test?"

"What's going on with you? You keep missing assignments. That's so not you, Claude."

I shook my head. "Daydreaming, I guess. So when is it?"

"Quiz tomorrow and test next Tuesday."

"Oh, right." I slapped my head like I'd forgotten the obvious.

"Thanks, Claude. I'd be lost without you."

"That's what Mom says."

Mom,

At group I told everyone that I wrote you a letter to tell you how proud I was of you for going to rehab. I would be if you'd gone. I was proud just before you had your final party and left me. I should have said something. I was just so sick of the relapses, though. I was so tired of it all.

While you were getting trashed with Gary, I was having dinner with the MacPhees and telling them that you'd been sober since spring and that this was the longest it had ever been and that I was sure you were cured. I was kind of bragging about you. I didn't shut up even when I knew I was exaggerating it all.

I can't stop thinking about that—how I wouldn't shut up about you. And at group I told them that you left a message saying you were doing well.

—Claude

* organize a binder for Liz

* get more soda

* clean car and fill up
  with gas

* work on application

* find more books for Liz

4

THE SCENT OF EARTH on Moonpie's paws woke me up. He kneaded my chest and thunked down on me. His diesel purr was as loud as Linwood's lobster boat. I wanted him to stay put. I didn't want to move anyway. My shoulders and arms ached like I'd been hauling traps or pulling weeds.

I stood under the shower and let the hot water melt my muscle aches and soothe the headache that was beginning at the back of my neck. I used the nailbrush on my dirty nails while the conditioner soaked into my hair. What had I done to myself? I put on jeans and a shirt and turned on the morning radio show. While the coffee brewed, I painted my fingernails Seashell Pink, and toenails, too. That would hide the dirt better, I thought.

It was while I was rushing around that I realized I could hurry off to the bus or I could take Mom's car. The car, of course. I took my mug and cereal, walked through the September flowers—asters, purple coneflowers, and cosmos—and up the stairs to the deck. From there I could see the ocean between the cottages. I sat with my feet on the railing and listened to birds in the trees and to the distant waves at low tide. A flash of yellow meant the bus had gone by, so I took a last gulp of coffee, but not before I noticed the mess the garden had become overnight. From the rooftop deck it looked as though something or someone had thrashed through it, leaving holes in the beds, bent stems, and crushed flowers.

Damn cat.

In English, after the quiz on poets of New England, I kept getting ideas for Liz's report. It was a flash of insight here, a memory from a book, or something I'd heard somewhere. The ideas kept coming. I wrote two pages of notes, and when class was over, I tore them out and handed them to Liz. It took her a second to figure out what it was, but when she did, she threw her arms around me.

"I love you, Claude. You saved me again." She hugged me tightly, and I didn't mind. I loved helping her because it helped me. I got a rush every time she learned something from me.

"I got another idea, too," I said as we walked down the hall. "I thought you could make a booklet of affirmations and what they mean and how they help you and—"

"Gotta go to class. Write that one down." She shuffled her books and tucked in a stray paper before she was gone around the corner.

I stopped and jotted the idea down in my notebook. I also decided I'd get her organized so that she could feel a little more pride in her work. All through my next class, I planned how I'd make the binder. I had an old one, and I'd put in paper, pocket folders, and dividers. I'd label her classes, and in the front pocket I'd tuck a Post-it pad. I'd surprise her.

Ms. Frost nabbed me on the way to lunch. "We need to set up a meeting to go over that scholarship."

We were in front of the Staff Lounge, where teachers and aides were eating lunch and hanging out. The odor of coffee and sweet muffins wafted out, and saliva pooled in my mouth. I swallowed. I hadn't brought a lunch.

"Sure, anytime," I said.

"Right now? We can have lunch in my office," she said. She looked at my armload of books. "Do you have a lunch?" When I shook my head, she said, "My treat."

We went down to the basement office and sat at a long rectangle table strewn with papers and a stapler. She handed me a yogurt and a banana, and she had the same. I couldn't take my eyes off the messy piles in the center of the table. Books were stacked in piles around the room, and psychology and education magazines littered the floor.

I couldn't believe a guidance counselor would work this way.

"Oh, let me move this stuff." She got up and began pushing it to one end of the table.

"I'll help," I said, separating the piles and neatening them up.

"Thank you, Claudine. I should be neater, but . . ." She shrugged. "It's not in me to care much about that sort of thing."

We ate our yogurts in silence for a minute. Her office smelled of sandalwood or musk or something. Whatever it was, I liked it. When I scanned the room, I saw a small brass bowl with an ash cone on her desk.

"You like that?" She left the spoon in her mouth and went to her desk and brought it back. "Take it with you. I have another."

I set it in front of me and turned it, studying the tiny lettering. "Thanks, I like it."

"I like the scent. Calms me down. It says, PEACE BE WITH YOU." She scraped the inside of her yogurt carton. "Now, let's talk about your mom."

I looked at the tiny incense bowl, imagining where I'd put it. Maybe I'd set it on the windowsill over the sink.

"You're still taking advantage of the group that meets at the Community Center? People with alcoholic family members need others they can talk to, people who understand what they're going through. So you know you're not alone."

"Oh, definitely, and now Liz goes with me." I could feel

her eyes on me, but still I turned the bowl. *Peace Be With You, Peace Be With You, Peace Be With You, Peace Be With You, Peace Be With You.*

"Is there anything else going on that I can help you with?"

"What do you think I should write for an essay?" I said.

She laughed and said, "Right. The scholarship. I think you should answer the question and say what's in your heart. If you don't show that you're serious, I guarantee they'll find someone else."

I nodded, but I actually didn't know what I'd say.

When Liz arrived after school, I had the notebook all ready for her on the coffee table. She plopped on the couch, and I sat on floor.

"Oh, Claude, that's sweet. You try and try, but I don't think you'll ever fix me." She laughed and flipped through the sections, fingering the Post-it flags.

"Just give it a try. Everything's easier if you have a system, Liz."

"Believe me, I've tried. My mom's tried, too. I'm just like Dad." She gave me a panicked look and then laughed.

"Don't worry, you're not your dad, Liz."

She flipped it open. "Let's label this section GREG LARA-MEE, and this one MATT."

I leaned back against the couch and took out the notes for the test.

"That was a joke, Claude. Loosen up." She nudged my elbow with her toe.

"Okay, it was funny. As long as you try to get organized."

She winked and gave a thumbs-up. "Gotcha."

"Keep looking. There's something else there."

She looked randomly until she came to the health section. "Oh my god, Claude."

"I only meant to do a little bit—notes and ideas, but I got going and I couldn't stop." I'd pretty much done the history of alcohol report for her. I'd covered the medicinal uses and abuses, even the expansion of twelve-step programs.

"You're an amazing friend." She read the first page, her finger tracing each line like she was in grade school again. I felt a tenderness toward her, like I was taking care of the little sister I'd never had.

"Claude," she said, slouching into the couch pillows, "I can't believe this. You do so much for me."

"It's okay, Liz, I don't mind."

She skimmed the next two pages. "Why do you . . . ? Nothing."

"What?" Did she want me to do more? I would if she needed the help. "I didn't add any of the drunk driving stuff, sorry."

"No, it's not that." She fanned through the sections.

"Let's study," I said. I shuffled the notes in the air. "Here's one he'll ask us: Define *metaphor*."

"I get it mixed up with the other one that uses *like* or *as*." She pushed the coffee table out and sat down on the floor next to me.

I flattened the notes to my chest. "You want the answer?"

She nodded.

"It's figurative language that uses one thing to describe another. For instance, to describe your dad, you might say, 'Dad's a ship on a stormy sea.'"

She pursed her lips. "Hmm. Nice, Claude." She took a long swig of soda and rubbed her hands together. "My turn now." She took the notes out of my hand. "What's a simile?"

"Definition: figurative language that describes something using *like* or *as*. Example: 'Mom is as brave as a soldier for going to rehab.'"

She nodded.

"Here's a metaphor," I said. "'Rehab is war on alcoholism.'"

"Very good." She wove her fingers together the way Mr. Springer did when he was talking about something serious. "Claudine, are you ready for when your mother comes back from Jackson Heights?"

I felt the blood drain from my face. "What?"

"Do you think you can pull back and not be so codependent? I mean, you practically did everything for her. From cleaning to driving to cooking to hiding her beer. Her recovery is personal."

My mouth opened to say something, but I couldn't find the words.

"Oh my god, Claude, you look like you're going to faint. I'm sorry. I've gotten so into this group and I read some of those books you gave me and I started thinking of how you've been your mother's keeper for so long and now she's going to be so different."

She leaned toward me with her arms out to hug me, knocking over her soda.

I was on my feet in a flash. "Shit, Liz! That's grape soda! I'll never get that out!" I ran to the cupboard under the sink. I was back with a sponge and some spray in seconds.

She apologized over and over, but I barely heard her. The soda was deep purple and would stain the sand-colored carpeting. It was old and didn't have a stain guard. No protection at all. I sprayed and wiped and sprayed and wiped until most of it was out. I left a film of cleaner on the spot to sink in overnight and put the bottle back.

"There," I said, sitting down again. "I'll let it sit for a while and go at it again later."

Liz, who was still holding the empty glass, stood over me and shook her head. "Hey, Claude, relax. It's just a spill." Her eyes had an expression she'd never shown me. It was a kind of pity, and it made me feel uneven, like I was rough around the edges.

I picked at my fingertips. "Right, Liz. No problem. Let's study now," I said, motioning her to sit. "Come on, sit down and I promise I'll forget about it."

Liz sat and shuffled her notes, but I had to be the one to get us going again. "How about personification? What's that?"

"I don't know. We've got time to get ready for this. Let's go out or something."

I snuck a peek at the stain. "I think I'll stay in and watch a movie or something."

"That sounds good." She bobbed her head in agreement. "Hey, Claudine, this is off topic, but do you think Matt's kind of cute?"

Matt. I thought of his slouch first. Then his curls, then his defiance. "Yeah, I do."

Later, in bed, I was thinking about the stain, not Matt. Then I was I remembering Liz's eyes. Her words came back and echoed in my head. *Relax. It's just a spill,* she'd said. Something burned under my skin, and I turned on my light. I held out my shaky hands. They were thin and scaly and red.

I found some lotion in the bathroom and rubbed it in, but it only burned like salt water in a cut. Cooling my hands under running water, I caught a glimpse of my white face in the mirror. Dark circles rimmed my red eyes. I threw water on my face and rubbed it until I had color. Then I scrubbed my hands for the umpteenth time that day.

In the living room I checked the stain. Liz didn't understand. I was responsible for this place. It was grape soda; of course I'd want to clean it up. I tucked my fists in my sleeves and closed my eyes, but all I could see was Liz's face, her eyes a blend of confusion and pity.

I had seen that look before, when Liz and I were in third grade. Our teacher, Miss Hart, announced that we'd be writing a play. A real play! Liz and I were so excited that we jumped up and down and hugged each other. For making too much noise, the teacher made us stay in and write it at recess time. I was fine with that, but Liz cried at the injustice and didn't do a thing to help. I secretly liked that she wouldn't be helping. The play was supposed to borrow from all the fairy tales we'd read: Cinderella, Hansel and Gretel, and all the others. Some kids wanted scary monsters; others wanted magic spells and witches. I knew exactly what to do. I'd write a princess story.

I sat at my desk, and Liz sat behind me with her head buried in her arms.

"You know what to do," Miss Hart said.

I smiled at her. My mind's screen was filled with ideas. My pink and yellow snow-globe princess appeared with a very big sword. I began to write. I called her Princess Courageous. She wore suitable clothes for the slaying of bad guys and whatever horrible things might come her way. Her family had disappeared, and she was in charge of the kingdom. Instead of telling the villagers that her parents were gone, she ran the kingdom by sending messages through her hawk, Nelson. She kept every monster, every criminal, and any other bad guys away with her sword. Of course, sometimes she had to kill, which she did with all the blood and gore necessary for such a job.

Miss Hart gasped and shook her head when she read it. "You'll have to write it over, Claudine."

"No," I said, stunned at my own bravery.

"There will be no violence in my classroom. Write it over for homework."

I took a corner of my paper and curled it around my pencil. "No," I said more quietly.

She bent close enough to me that I could smell her lipstick and coffee breath. "You should know better than anyone that the world needs nice stories."

Why? I wondered. And how would I know better than other kids? It was my turn to cry, and I wanted Mom.

When I got home, I took my story into her room, where she was curled up in bed. The room was dark except for a bedside light. I got under the covers with her and checked out the gardening magazine she was reading. Dried flowers. Boring. I explained what had happened.

"Mom, I don't get what she meant by, 'You should know better than anyone.'"

"I don't get it either, Angel. Just do it over," she said. She put her arm around me and blew a smoke ring. I put my finger through it.

"It's about Princess Courageous."

"Make her put out a fire and be done with it." She smoothed my hair from my eyes.

"I make up stories with my snow globe every night so I can get to sleep." I put her free hand back on my head so she'd stroke my hair.

"Really, now." She took a deep drag on her cigarette, the kind where you can watch the ash grow longer and the white paper get shorter.

"When you were a kid, did you make up stories, too?"

Her hand froze on my head. "I don't remember much about when I was a kid." She leaned back and closed her eyes. "You ought to get rid of that thing. That's a baby toy. Nobody does stuff like that in third grade anyways."

I left her smoking in bed and marched off to my room and shut the door. The snow globe sat on the bedside table. I tipped it over and back and watched while the white flakes swirled around Princess Courageous and settled at her feet. She didn't look so magical anymore; she was a yellow and pink plastic girl with eyes too blue, standing on a green hill. That night I wrote a nice play where the princess was saved by a handsome prince and everyone was good and happy. Liz was relieved, and the teacher looked relieved, too.

Dear Mom,

I was thinking of my snow globe, and I guess I never told you what I did that night you told me it was a baby toy and to get rid of it.

Well, I went out behind the workshop and dug a hole deep enough for the princess and buried her.

Man, I was pissed at you for making me feel so stupid. Because of that, I suddenly understood the black-and-whiteness of you. One day I'm a princess, the next day—no, the next second I'm an angel, then I'm your baby, and then I'm a brat. What am I tonight, Mom?

I've dug it up, all that old anger. I'm pissed about that snow globe all over again.

—Claudine

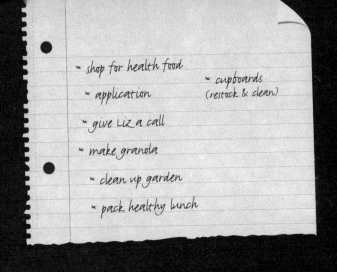

- shop for health food
  - application
- give Liz a call
- make granola
  - clean up garden
  - pack healthy lunch

* cupboards
  (restock & clean)

5

L IZ CAME LATE TO LUNCH. Her eye makeup was smeared. Her face was splotchy, and her nostrils were red-rimmed. She sat covering her face, cell phone clutched in one hand. She would've cried longer if I hadn't taken the phone and set it down. She let out a squeal.

"Hey, talk to me," I said.

She began to sob. "Mom just called," she said, grabbing the phone. "Dad's gone. He took off last night."

"He hasn't come home?"

"No. Poor Mom. She never said anything this morning, but now she wants me to come home as soon as I can."

I hugged her and let her cry awhile. It felt good to be

able to help. "Don't freak out. He'll probably be home by the time school's out."

She nodded and wiped her nose. "Mom sounds calm. Too calm. You know?"

"Yeah, I know."

"Maybe I should go home now. What if he gets in a car accident—what if he hits someone?"

The cafeteria sounds were building as more kids arrived. I leaned in toward her. "Let's think this through. Is there anything you can possibly do to change it?" She shook her head and tore at her tissue. "Your mom said there's no news, right?" She nodded. "Will it help your dad if you miss your classes?" She smiled a little and shook her head. "Let's finish the day and then give your mom another call."

"But Mom said—"

"But nothing. You need to take care of you."

She nodded. "Thanks, Claude."

We walked side by side down the hall. "I'm sorry about your dad, Liz." Something about her made me want to protect her.

As soon as the dismissal bell rang at the end of the day, I went to my locker. Liz waved her cell phone at me from across the hall and motioned to the door. I was anxious to get home and work on the list of chores. I had a wash to do and cupboards to rearrange. There would be no more crap in the house, only healthy food. Instead of chips, there'd be bread and cheese, vegetables and fruit. Instead of soda, there'd be juice, tea, and maybe coffee. I had to think about that one. The health food brainstorm had come in gym class when the teacher talked about the effect that nutrition had on our thinking. Sugar gives extreme energy but sends you crashing. I thought a nutrition overhaul might help me with the shaky feeling I was having.

When I came out the front doors, Liz was sitting on the steps waiting for me. I sat next to her. "How'd it go?"

She smiled big and said, "He's back, and he wants to talk to Mom and me." She covered her face and screamed into her hands.

"Are you okay?"

She was fine. She was grinning all over. "Sorry. That was a happy scream. I'm glad he's not dead, I guess."

I scratched at the mica flecks in the steps. She nudged me.

"What?" I said, nudging her back.

"It hasn't been easy for you either," she said.

"No . . ."

"Have you heard from your Mom?"

I closed my eyes. "Just that message."

"You ought to send her a letter."

I thought of the letters in the back of the notebook. "She's not ready for those quite yet," I said.

"No, don't send her any of those. A regular letter, you know."

I nodded and picked more mica chips.

"You coming?" She stood up and grabbed both my backpack and hers.

"To group? We can't ditch it?"

"No. Not today."

Lydia was putting the folding chairs in a circle when we arrived. Blake was following behind setting a clipboard down on each one. Matt and Deb laughed about something at the other end of the room, and Cindy and Hanna sat quietly side by side, each in her own world.

"Okay, time." Lydia set her coffee on an empty chair beside her. "If you need me, I'm here. Otherwise the floor is yours. Who wants to start us?"

Liz raised her hand. "Me, I'd like to share."

"Okay, Liz," Lydia said.

"My name's Liz, and I'm the daughter of an alcoholic." She bit her lip.

"Hi, Liz," we said.

"My father hit bottom. Last night he took off when he was drunk. He didn't come back until this afternoon." She looked at me. "Claudine helped me get through a hard day. I couldn't have done it without you, Claude."

"It's okay," I said. I was shocked at her honesty, the way she easily spilled her guts to them.

"Dad wants to talk to Mom and me when I get home. I'm not sure what to do or say."

"Just take it one day at a time, Liz," Deb said.

"Right. You can't cure him; you can only take care of yourself," Hanna said.

Liz nodded. "Well, he's definitely out of the Pleasure Zone now. I can't trust him anymore."

"Pleasure Zone?" Lydia said.

"Yeah, the P.Z. Dad used to handle it okay. You know, not too drunk and not too sober. His Pleasure Zone. But now he can't control it. He's crashing." Liz started to tear up. "It was bad last night; he acted just like a *real* drunk." The room grew silent. Except for an occasional sniff from Liz, nobody spoke.

Mom always acted like a real drunk, but Liz's dad could be smashed and function at the same time. I was always jealous of that. I tried to catch her eye, but she wasn't looking anywhere but at her clipboard, where a pool of tears had collected.

"You knew it was a myth that alcoholics could control their drinking," Hanna said. "You knew it, right?"

"Yeah, but like I said, I didn't think he was a real drunk. I guess—" She blew her nose. "I guess I thought he was different. Better."

Matt let out a dramatic sigh and stretched his legs. "You mean better dressed."

Deb laughed and kicked Matt's boot.

"Matt, that was so low," Cindy said. She clucked her tongue and shook her head. "Low."

"Well, yeah, sorry. I'm just so sick of people not saying what they think. When my old man gets smashed, I just tell him off and leave. When he sobers up, I come back. Simple. You can't do nothin' about it," Matt said. "Why's everyone so friggin' polite all the time?"

"I've never told him what I think about his drinking," Liz said. "It wasn't a big deal until this year."

"I didn't talk with my parents at first either," Cindy said. "But you'll find out it can be rewarding to share your feelings. I did with my parents, and we all cried and now we share all the time."

I stayed as still as possible. I didn't want to be in this conversation.

Matt said, "That's a crock. You think that's how it works for everybody? We all cry and then have a group hug?" He threw up his hands. "You realize that you sound excruciatingly superior?"

Cindy looked pale.

He sat on the edge of his seat. "People, listen to me. The reality is that you can't trust a drunk with your feelings."

Lydia cleared her throat. *Here it comes,* I thought, *she'll take over.* But it was just that: throat clearing.

Matt was right about the trust thing, but I wasn't in the sharing mood. I wanted to disappear.

Friday night was mall night, but Liz announced that she was going to spend it with her family, since her dad was going through a bad time. That was good—I wanted to spend some time rearranging the kitchen. After stocking up on groceries at High Tide Health Foods, I dove into a cleaning frenzy. In the kitchen I reorganized the fridge and threw away anything that was opened and anything that could be thought of as junk food. I wiped down the counters and cupboards and restocked them with oats, wheat berries, whole-wheat pastry flour, dried fruits, and pastas.

I consulted my list on the fridge door. It said: *Clean the toilet and sink.* I scrubbed away at the rust stains, but nothing helped. I poured bleach into the toilet bowl and washed my hands in the sink. Goose bumps rose on my forearms as hot water pounded my hands. I felt someone near me, but it couldn't be true—I'd locked the door. I looked in the mirror. Nobody. Just me, a pale, thin stranger with a halo of something white behind my head. Was it someone's clothing, hair, scarf? I had to look. I counted *one, two, three, four, five,* and turned. Of course, a towel. It hung on the door, used and unfolded. That should teach me to be neater.

Even though it had only been a towel, I was still jumpy when the phone rang. Before I picked it up, I turned on the TV so I'd have some background noise after I hung up.

"Claude, you were awesome today."

"Thanks, Liz. But, awesome?"

"You were there when I needed you."

"Thanks. How's it going with your dad?"

"He's sorry, and he says he's got a drinking problem."

"Really? He's brilliant."

"Yep. He even cried. It was hard to see him like that."

"Big, tough Tom MacPhee?"

"And he's going to go to meetings and maybe to Jackson Heights."

My throat closed up and I couldn't breathe.

"Claude?"

I forced myself to breathe through my nose while I held the phone to my pounding heart. I was dizzy with the effort and tried to swallow, which made me cough. I gasped and took a breath.

"Claude! Are you okay?"

"Right here," I said, panting.

"Maybe you ought to take a day off. You haven't been looking so hot lately."

"I just had something in my throat. I'm fine."

That night I couldn't sleep. I puffed up my bed with extra pillows and blankets, thinking I needed to be more comfortable. Something was nagging away at me. I felt the way an oyster from the cove feels when a grain of sand gets between its soft body and its shell home. After so much irritation, it creates a little pearl. I went over and over the meeting at the Community Center. What was irritating me? Maybe I was just creating a pearl.

I finally fell asleep half sitting, half lying down with Moonpie on my shoulder.

I jerked awake with a heavy feeling of dread. Something was wrong. I looked around, touching my cheek where I'd felt a whisper of something. Had someone called my name? Nobody was there. Moonpie was gone. The night was bright enough to make shadows of sunflowers and cosmos on my floor. Out my window, the moon hung over the workshop like an overripe melon.

I picked up the cat, who was waiting by the door, and went down the steps to the garden path in my underwear and T-shirt. The shells were sharp, and I tiptoed as I made my way to the center raised bed. I heard the whoosh of a car on Sea Road and then the pounding of the surf. Moonpie squirmed out of my arms and into the catnip patch. He rubbed up against the long stems and rolled to the ground.

A twig broke, and I stiffened. "Is someone here?" My voice sounded thin and raspy. "Don't hide."

Snap!

Moonpie had rolled again and broken off a stem of catnip. "Goddamned cat! You scared the hell out of me." He flattened his ears and ran off. I threw a shell after him and went back inside.

I stayed up and rearranged the cupboards so that the cereal goods would be right next to the fridge. While I wiped down the counter, I thought of something else I had never let Mom know.

Dear Mom,

I never told you about the time I wet the bed. I was about seven years old, and the police had been at the trailer that night because of a noise complaint. When they came, I didn't know it was the police. There were no sirens or blinking lights. I just remember how the party noise changed from laughter and fun in the living room to swearing and bottles being gathered up and the stereo being turned low. I opened my bedroom door a crack to see what was going on, and two big guys in uniforms were in the middle of the living room. They were so clean. Not a wrinkle or a speck of dirt on either of them; their buttons and badges and shoes were so shiny. One turned around and tipped his hat at me. I shut my door and ran back into bed. A few minutes later my door opened and he stood there in the doorway. He didn't move, and he didn't say anything. I didn't either. I just lay still as a statue, holding my breath, quiet as a rabbit. As soon as he shut the door, I let out a huge breath and flooded the bed with pee I didn't know I'd been holding. I was surprised by the heat of it, and then surprised by the coolness of it when I threw off the covers to see what I'd done.

Later, when I heard the car doors slamming and your bedroom door shut, I carried my sheets and pajamas out to the backyard and dug a hole and buried them.

I never told anyone. Not you, not Liz. Nobody.

I've been holding that in for a long time.

—Claudine

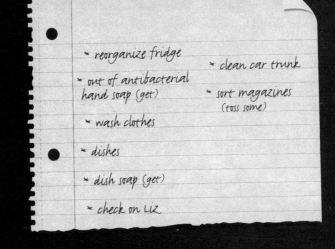

* reorganize fridge
* out of antibacterial
  hand soap (get)
* wash clothes
* dishes
* dish soap (get)
* check on Liz

* clean car trunk
* sort magazines
  (toss some)

6

THE FIRST THING THAT ANNOYED ME Saturday morning was the sloppy stacks of magazines on the coffee table. It was a mess again, and I had vowed to keep it neat and organized. *The whole place could use some help,* I thought. I started with the oven. It had brown stains from cooking French fries and fish. I moistened some steel wool and got it soapy. On my knees I scrubbed until the speckled pattern showed once again. I wiped it clean. It gleamed.

Once, when Mom and Linwood had a bunch of friends over to party, she'd told them that I was her maid. I think I was around seven years old.

"Look—I got her trained," Mom said, throwing a handful of chips on the floor. I rushed over and picked them up and put them on the table like it was a big emergency. Everyone cracked up. I smiled a little. I was a good girl, and they could see that.

I started to walk away, but then Candy tipped over her beer. I ran to the sink and got a roll of paper towels, knelt down, and mopped it up while they laughed over me.

An ashtray dropped beside the beer. "See if she'll take care of that," someone said.

"No doubt," Mom said. "She can't let anything go. She's a regular Heloise."

They roared as the ashes dissolved in the watery mess. I worked as fast as I could, but one by one, the rest of the group added to the pile until I had a mound of beer, pizza crusts, chips, butts, and soda. I kept my mind on the task. If I sniffed, they'd know I was crying, so I let my snot drip onto the mess. I kept my head down and blocked them out. *Eyes on the floor,* I told myself. *Eyes on the floor.* I got the broom and silently loaded the whole pile onto a pizza carton. By the time I spilled it into the garbage can, the laughing had stopped and an eerie silence filled the room.

"Weird," someone said.

"She's always been like this." Mom leaned toward me. "You can't stand the clutter, right, baby angel?"

I kept my head down to hide my running nose.

"Candy, you wanna borrow her?" Mom asked.

"No thanks, Serena. She's a little twisted."

"Hey, watch it. I love her." Mom grabbed my arm and pulled me to her. "Right, Princess?" My wet face was buried in her dark, wavy hair. It smelled of her vanilla musk and cigarette smoke. She squeezed me hard, and I stiffened. I wiped the snot from her hair and went to my room for the rest of the night.

I shook off the memory. In the living room I looked more closely at the three piles of magazines. I'd divided them equally by topic: *Cosmo, Better Homes and Gardens, People.* For good measure I arranged them left to right in order of importance: *Better Homes and Gardens, People, Cosmo.* Perfect. Except, beside *Cosmo* was something tiny. I held it close. My stomach turned over in recognition. It was a small silver loop. Mom's toe ring. I went through the past few days and tried to remember if I'd set it there. I knew I hadn't, and my stomach flipped over again. But Liz had sat right there, and she might have found it and set it beside the magazines.

I wanted out. I got in the car. At the mailbox I grabbed five days' worth of overflowing mail. I dropped the heap in the passenger seat and wrote out a Post-it reminding me to get the mail every day.

It was mostly junk, but two were bills for phone and power and another was a slim envelope with a shiny window and the name SERENA M. CARBONNEAU peeking out. In the upper left corner was the familiar address. My hands trembled. "Yes!" I said to no one.

I looked in the mirror. With a snap, I unclasped my barrette and let down my hair. Mom's dark lipstick was in the glove compartment. Instant transformation.

I got in line at the drive-through window on the far side

of the bank. I signed the welfare check and put it in the vacuum tube.

"Hey, Serena. Cash or checking?" the speaker said.

Shit, who was that? "Oh, all cash please." It was impossible to see through the other car windows to the person talking, but I waved anyway.

The tube landed with a smack outside my window.

"Don't spend it all in one place!"

I parked in the power company parking lot and stuffed a fat envelope with two months of late payments. I did the same with the phone bill. I dropped each payment in the night depository boxes at their billing offices. It was a good feeling, like when all the socks in the laundry pair up perfectly.

I drove along the shore, watching the horizon line, imagining Mom in rehab. Blue lights flashing froze me behind the wheel. My heart hammered in my chest. I pulled over.

"Miss," an officer said, tapping on the glass.

I rolled down the window.

"License and registration, please."

I took them from the glove compartment and handed them to him.

"Do you know why I pulled you over, Miss Serena Carbonneau?" he asked, ducking down to see my face.

Tears appeared from nowhere, and I blinked them onto my cheeks. I looked up at his mirrored sunglasses and through the blur I saw Mom looking back at me. I couldn't turn away.

He patted the roof. "Your back left taillight is out. You'll have to signal manually until you get it fixed." He waited for a reaction, then smiled, handing back the license and registration. "Registration is due next month, too. On your way, then." He gave a nod. "And drive safely."

I crept away from the side of the road, both hands clamped to the steering wheel, watching the cop in my rearview mirror sitting in his car, talking into his radio, getting smaller and smaller. "Only a taillight, only a taillight. Remember to signal." I counted cars as they passed: *One, two, three, four, five, one, two, three, four, five.*

I drove around the beach and up to town and back down again until somehow I was in the MacPhees' driveway. I could smell the grill and guessed it was burgers. Brandy barked and came running from around back, with Liz just behind. She leaned into the driver's seat window.

"Are you here to rescue me? Please?"

"I was just out and wondered how you were doing," I said.

She rolled her eyes. "You've gotta save me. Dad's smothering me with love. He wants to be sure I forgive him, so today is all about the family. Frisbee, burgers, and togetherness." She tugged on my hair. "You look like your mom with your hair down. Come eat and we'll make a plan."

I walked around back with her, Brandy licking at my hand. I wiped it on my pants.

Mr. MacPhee stood up, spatula in one hand, soda in the other. "Claudina, my girl. Long time." He gave me a kiss on the cheek and opened the grill lid with the spatula. He hadn't called me that nickname in a while. I secretly loved it, even though I claimed to hate it.

"Hey, Tomasina," I said.

"Ah, you remembered. Please join us. There's tons to eat. Tons."

I waved to Mrs. MacPhee, who was on the chaise looking pissed off but glamorous in her Jackie Onassis sunglasses. She waved back but didn't say anything.

"Is your mom okay?" I whispered to Liz.

"Shell-shocked, but she'll be fine."

We got sodas and moved over to the patio. "So, Dad told us he'd been drinking more and now he knows it's time to cut back. If the meetings aren't enough, he wants to look into Jackson Heights, too."

The condensation on the can was slimy under my hand, and I wiped it on my jeans. "Yeah, you told me."

"Isn't that great?"

I took a sip. It was too sweet. "I need some water, Liz."

She fished for a bottled water in the cooler. "It went pretty well."

My hands were sticky with dog drool. I had to wash them. "I'll be right back," I said, and went into her kitchen. I filled my palms with blue liquid dish soap and let the water get hot before I rubbed my hands into a lather. I rinsed and did it again. Brandy panted at the door, strings of drool dangling from his jowls. "I don't think so, dog." I shook off the water and dried my hands with a paper towel.

From the sink I could see into the living room, where

Mrs. MacPhee had her collection of crystal figurines. I looked around the corner. My stomach did a flip, and I remembered a sleepover we had in that living room in front of the Christmas tree. The tree reached all the way up to the second-floor balcony.

I heard Mr. MacPhee ask Liz to get the condiments, so I stepped back into the kitchen. She came in and got ketchup, relish, and mustard from the fridge. "What do you want to do after we eat?"

"Anything," I said.

We spent the afternoon at the beach, sitting on the hood of the car, getting the last of the sun and hanging with whoever stopped by. But then Jenna Carver came over, and the energy changed. She was convinced that the three of us should go to the after-football-game party that her brother Jake was throwing at her house. Liz agreed, and they hopped in the car. "Come on, Claude," Liz said. "You're driving."

Out the open window, Jenna said, "Jake was awesome. You should've gone. They slaughtered them. Don't you ever go to the games?"

I shook my head and hopped in.

Jenna said, "I love football. Jake's going to introduce me to Ryan. You know, the quarterback? He's hot. So hot."

Liz and I locked eyes. She looked into the back at Jenna. "Jenna, take a breath," she said.

Jenna giggled. "I can't help it. I'm so pumped up."

"Oh my god," I mouthed.

Jenna hollered out the window as I pulled into her driveway. There were people pouring in and out of her house, and the music was pumping from speakers placed in the open windows. She hopped out and jumped on her brother's back. "Jakey!" Liz was right behind her.

I stayed in the car, hand on the key. My fingers wouldn't move. Fear tightened my belly, and I looked behind me. Another car was blocking me in. I'd be blocked in.

"Come on," Liz called. "Her parents gave them the house for the night."

I shifted into reverse and backed the car around the oncoming car and out of the driveway.

On the way home I kept the windows open and the music off. The trailer was dark and peaceful. The only light was the message light blinking. It was Liz and Jenna saying that a couple of guys wanted to know who the babe with the long, funky hair was.

"They like the new look, Claude. Keep the lipstick. And COME BACK!" They hooted and whooped into the phone and hung up with a bang.

I went into the bathroom and showered off the lipstick and everything else. In order for my hair to not look as kinky as Mom's, I had to condition it a lot. I gooped it with an extra handful of Hot Body and wrapped it in a towel. While it soaked in, I painted Night Rose Red over my Seashell Pink toes and watched the History Channel. I rested my feet on the coffee table and closed my eyes. Whenever they shut, I saw Mom. Her shocked expression, her pleading eyes, her hair in clumps.

I fumbled for the remote and turned up the volume. Beside my right foot was Mom's toe ring. I touched my second toenail. It was dry. I slipped it around my toe. Cool. The silver was perfect with the red.

I opened my notebook to my section of letters.

Dear Mom,

All of a sudden I can't stop looking back. It's like I cracked open a door and now memories are leaking out. Today without warning I remembered the birthday parties you ruined, and I keep remembering the way Mrs. MacPhee would make a big deal about my "special day" and I would come home with presents from her on my birthday. It's true that sometimes you'd remember, but sometimes you didn't. I never told you that she bought me those winter boots I had in fourth grade. I didn't get them from the lost and found at school—the jacket either. Didn't you think it was weird that Liz and I matched like twin sisters?

Here's something I forgot until I was at Liz's today. You never knew that when I went over there, I took things from Mrs. MacPhee's makeup drawers in the bathroom. I stole things, Mom. You never noticed the new stuff? The extra-fancy soaps in the bathroom? Soaps in different shapes, perfume samples, complimentary shampoos from the Marriott, a folding hairbrush?

There is a shelf in their living room that has crystal figurines that Mr. MacPhee brought back from business trips for Mrs. MacPhee. There was a wren that was posed like it was going to take flight. Every time I passed through that room I checked on that wren. I was obsessed with it, and one night when I slept over, I stuck it in my pocket. No one noticed that I had anything in my pocket, and nobody noticed it was gone.

I wish I hadn't remembered that. I want to close the door.

When I started stealing, I didn't do it all at once. I took one thing each time, until one day Liz noticed that the rose-shaped guest soaps in our bathroom were just like the ones at her house. She trusts me so much that it doesn't occur to her that I'd done anything wrong.

I never did it again after the soap incident, and I buried all of it in the backyard so you'd never know.

—Claude

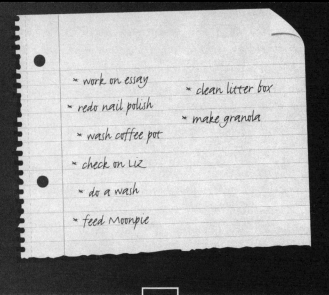

* work on essay
* redo nail polish
* wash coffee pot
* check on Liz
* do a wash
* feed Moonpie
* clean litter box
* make granola

7

I was one big ache when I woke up. I could have sworn *I* was the football player, not Jenna's brother. My body was curled up, and I was on my side. When I remembered it was Sunday, I went back to sleep.

I woke for real when light slanted onto my bedroom floor. That meant it was afternoon. Moonpie was at the front door, waiting patiently for me to let him out.

It was when I reached for the door handle that I noticed my fingernails. They were dirty red stubs. Most of the polish was chipped off. Didn't I just paint these? What had happened? In the shower I dug into what was left of my nails until it hurt too much to clean them. Later I could use a nailbrush on them, and then all I'd need is a little more polish.

The phone rang while I was drying off. I let the machine pick up. It was Liz and Jenna telling me everything I'd missed, and did I want to meet at the beach to play Frisbee with the football team? I walked to the machine and clicked it off. It sounded like a nightmare.

I spread the application out on the kitchen table again and looked over the first five pages. The sun glared at me through the kitchen window. I pulled the shade. The first page was done. The second page wanted my school history and my grades. That was easy: straight As. I reread the first page:

APPLICANT: CLAUDINE MARIE CARBONNEAU
ADDRESS: 2 SEA SPRAY ACRES, DEEP COVE, MAINE
BIRTHPLACE: PORTLAND, MAINE

I sat down and put the papers in order. I left the space for FATHER empty. I finished Mom's information the best I could.

MOTHER'S NAME: SERENA MARIE CARBONNEAU

A space for Mom's birthplace was next. It was someplace in Wisconsin or something. That doesn't mean it was her home. She and Grandma moved around a lot.

I set the five pages back in their folder and lifted the kitchen shade. The sun pierced my eyes, and I turned away. I pulled every shade in the trailer and made it dark, like when I was young—shades drawn, and only fingers of light touching the rooms. If there'd been blue, hazy cigarette smoke hanging in the air and Mom at the kitchen table, I'd be twelve years old again.

I needed to do the essay, but instead I wrote to Mom.

Dear Mom,

I almost went to a party yesterday—for about two minutes. I just about threw up and all I did was smell the beer. No, all I did was SEE the beer. I ran home to Moonpie. I ran, but not like you do. I think my running was a good kind of running away.

Your running away is just a geographic cure (as they say in group), and soon you'll be tired of Gary. You know how I preached to you and you never listened? Well, get this—it's important. The geographic cure really isn't the best thing, you know. People who run away just to escape their problems are only half right. They KNOW they have a problem and that they need to get away from it. BUT they move WITH the problem instead of leaving it. They carry it with them, on their backs, along with all their luggage. You know why? The problem is more than the six-packs they left behind in the fridge or the guys they're running from. The problem is inside them. Their souls are sick, and you can't leave your soul behind in the fridge or pour it down the drain.

The books say you need to start by admitting you have a problem and then you need to work from the inside out. There are six-packs all over America, and Gary isn't going to save you from that. This is just denial in a big geographic, cross-country way.

Mr. MacPhee is thinking of going to Jackson Heights. It was my dream for you to do rehab, but now it won't happen, and it's a little weird that Liz's dad is going to the place I said you're at. Not just weird, but wrong. It should be you going there, not him!!

Damn you, Mom. It could've been you if you'd just tried a little harder.

—Claude

be spontaneous

write Mom

clean car

call Liz

organize a Frisbee game

work on the essay

organize morning routine

8

A T SCHOOL I COULDN'T PAY ATTENTION to Mr. Springer, and Liz kept poking me.

"You look sick, Claude. What's wrong with you?"

I pushed my hair back from my face and looked at the board. Springer had made a graphic organizer of a poem. It was in the shape of a tree.

"Claudine, you're good with these things. What's your input?"

Wisps of hair floated down again. They weren't really wisps, but greasy strands. With a shock I realized that I hadn't showered that morning. Had I taken one yesterday? I couldn't remember. Yesterday I'd shut the shades and stayed inside. My face flamed red.

"I don't know, Mr. Springer," I said.

"Were you listening?"

I nodded. While he went on about how each word balances on the next, I wondered where I'd been. I knew I'd worked on my application and written to Mom. Did I go to bed? Of course, here I was. I looked at my shirt. I'd worn it yesterday.

Mr. Springer's voice reached into my thoughts. "There's nothing wasted, not one word. Each one is as important as the rest," he said. "Now, what about the other poets? Do you feel the same way?"

I tried to pay attention, but all I could see were the greasy strands that dangled before my eyes. I wouldn't have been surprised if the group called out names like when I was little. *Hey, Stinky!*

I squeezed my hands tighter. My knuckles turned white, a contrast to the dirt in the creases. A shot of adrenaline spiked through my body. My hands were dirty. I curled them into fists and stood up. "Excuse me," I said, weaving in and out of the tables toward the door.

The halls were empty, so I ran to the girls' room. Mirrors don't lie. What happened to me? My hair was my best feature, and now it was skanky. I finger-combed my long hair and twisted it into a neat knot. Under hot water, I scrubbed my hands and dug the dirt from under my nails. My skin grew redder under the hot water and the school soap stung, but the pain meant it was cleaning out the germs. I held my cupped palms under the powerful stream and planned the shower I'd have when I got home. I'd run it steaming hot and get out all the puffs and scrubs and every kind of body wash we had. I'd breathe deeply and cleanse my lungs, too.

How could I forget to take a shower? It wouldn't happen again. Never again. I'd put a Post-it in every room if I had to.

The girls' room door swung open, and Liz came in. "You okay?" she asked.

"Yeah, fine," I said, adding more soap. "I must've overslept."

She scrunched up her face—her confused look.

"I didn't get a shower. Just wanted to wash up a bit." I splashed my face and blew out a long breath. I wiped the steamed-up mirror with my hand. Better. My reflection was more alive.

Liz turned off the hot water. "Jesus, Claude, you're gonna burn yourself."

She looked at me like I was crazy.

"I'm better now," I said, taking a paper towel and patting my hands and face.

She followed me out. "You're being weird. Weird!"

As we came in, Mr. Springer said, "Tomorrow's the test. Be ready."

I opened my notebook with a smack. Test taking was a snap. Ace in the hole.

"You'll answer a few questions in essay form, do some matching, fill in the blanks, and I'll have some extra-credit opportunities," he said.

I arranged my notes across my desk and sat waiting.

Liz stood up and hoisted her backpack over her shoulder. "What are you doing? The test is tomorrow. Time for group."

Lydia sat forward in her chair. Her auburn hair splayed out over her shoulders, reminding me of the seaweed that washed up on the shore of Deep Cove.

"I was thinking about Liz's term, the Pleasure Zone. I like the way it describes her dad's misconception about his alcoholism. And I want to tell Liz and Claudine how I admire that they're talking about it in their homes. That's an opportunity not everyone feels they have."

I felt myself flush deep red, and I wished I was home in my shower cleaning off the crud that showed. My hair was pulled back, but it was greasy.

"You know, I have my own Pleasure Zone," Matt said.

"Ooo, and don't I know it," Deb said. She cracked herself up and had to turn away to get it together. I took the opportunity to force a deep breath and breathe it out slowly. I picked at my nails and focused on the shiver it gave me as I peeled away the ends of my thumbnails.

Matt stuck out his long legs and crossed them. "You wish, Deb. But if you play your cards right . . . maybe." He winked at her. "But I really do have a Pleasure Zone, and it's not what you think. It's when Dad's doing his thing—drinking—and I'm doing mine—ignoring it. It's fine. We accept it all without making it a big deal, but it's not real. In the back of my mind, I know it can't last. I know it's coming. It's building, and pretty soon, BAM!" He smacked his hands together, and I jumped in my seat. "Sorry, Claude. I guess you know what I mean."

"No," I said, too fast and too defensively. Everyone turned and looked. I was red in the face again.

Blake said, "So the Pleasure Zone is a perceived control."

Chris laughed. "Man, you're such a geek."

"He's right," Deb said, "exactly right. It's like after a big fight and you've made up. Things are balanced just so, but you haven't really talked it out. You think it's all fine again because it looks good on the outside, but things can only last so long that way before, BAM! You have to deal with it all again."

Feet shuffled, positions changed, and throats cleared. Silence grew until Lydia asked, "So why doesn't the Pleasure Zone work?"

"It's what Matt said," I said. "You know something worse is coming."

"Did you know your mother's relapse was coming?" Blake asked.

I looked up in shock. "It wasn't really a relapse. Not like the others."

That was a lie. It was exactly like the others.

Liz turned to me, and I felt her gaze on me.

"It was worse because I thought she was recovered." A lump rose in my throat.

Matt nodded to me and looked away.

Steam rose from the bottom of the shower stall, and I was wrapped in a blanket of clean, warm clouds. My face flushed, but it wasn't from shame, it was from the purge, the filth oozing from my pores. The water pounded me clean, and I watched all of the grease from the day whirl down the drain.

There had been a commercial when I young that sang about the squeaky clean sound you get from clean hair. I washed my hair over and over until I got that sound and then I washed it again and again. I washed it five times and then conditioned it. I held my palms out to see if I was done. My skin was pink and my fingers were tender prunes. A new beginning.

As I dried off, Matt's voice echoed in my ears. Even though I hadn't wanted to listen today, something replayed, uninvited. *Does everyone have a Pleasure Zone?* What about Mom and me? Ours was always the summer.

I wiped the steam from the mirror. I combed my hair out and didn't like what I saw. The hair that had hung in my eyes today had to be cut. Without giving it another thought, I took the scissors from the shelf and snipped straight across. There. Now I had bangs. The frizz at the ends? I lopped off a couple of inches, and it was gone. I set the scissors down on the shelf and went to find Post-its.

I had a large supply for school, and I was proud of the system I used for studying. Everything had a color. Blue was for history, red for English, green for science, yellow for math, and so on. Within those subjects, I had another system. I'd flag the pages that were important, then stick a Post-it on the page, making the notes that I needed right there.

I opened the heavy notebook and unzipped the nylon pocket that held the Post-its. The dividers were empty. Every Post-it flag had been ripped off. A thumping began in my chest. An image of the colored flags popped into my mind. I saw myself lining them up on the edge of the library table while I talked to Liz. *What an idiot.* I couldn't have another day like today; I had to get organized. I needed a new system. I needed more than one kind of Post-it.

The first Post-it I wrote was: *fix your notebook.* Then I wrote: *set the alarm.* I stuck it on the bathroom mirror. Then I wrote: *you took a shower today.* I stuck it right under the other note. In every room, I left a reminder for myself to take a shower. Later, when I cleaned Mom's car and I noticed the gas gauge on E, I left a Post-it on the dashboard: *get gas.*

With each Post-it, the tension eased a bit, the clamp loosened. I was creating a calmness around me. I was in control. I could sleep now.

First I wrote to Mom. It was getting to be a ritual. Or a confessional.

Dear Mom,

I was always jealous of the kids at school that got picked up by their parents to go on vacations or even to the doctor's office. One day I wrote a note that said: "Dear Mrs. Trescott, Claudine has a 2:30 appointment at Dr. Hall's across the street. Please allow her to leave at 2:25 and walk there. Thank you for being a good

teacher to my little girl. Sincerely, Serena Carbonneau."
Mrs. Trescott didn't even blink. I left at 2:25 and hid
behind the dentist's office until the buses lined up outside the school. Then I went home like always. It wasn't
what I expected. Nobody asked how it was—if I had a
cavity or needed braces. I had to offer up the story to
whoever would listen. Liz was there to listen.

"I have two cavities, and I need braces, too."

Liz opened her eyes wide. "Wow, Claude. When do
you get them?"

"My mom won't let me get them, I know."

"Lucky you."

—Claude

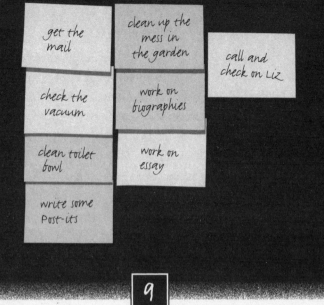

get the
mail

clean up the
mess in
the garden

call and
check on Liz

check the
vacuum

work on
biographies

clean toilet
bowl

work on
essay

write some
Post-its

9

I WAS JOLTED OUT OF MY SLEEP by Mrs. MacPhee's
voice on the answering machine. "Don't forget the
baskets, Claudine. Even though your mother doesn't attend
the Boosters Club meetings, she can still contribute to our
cause. We're raising money for band uniforms. And I think
it's great that your mom is doing what she's doing. Come
on over and visit us again sometime."

Did she really think Mom was so stupid? The last
thing Mom would ever support was the school band. She
never even graduated. I lifted Moonpie off my chest and
stared at the muddy paw prints he'd left on my T-shirt. A
cold breeze blew through the trailer, and the storm door

slammed open and closed. I wrote a Post-it to drop off a few of Mom's baskets at the MacPhees.

In the kitchen, the fridge hummed and the baseboard ticked. I still had time for breakfast. A pink Post-it was stuck to the coffeemaker. It said: *check the vacuum*. The Post-its were saving me from a lot of potential problems. I went to the broom closet and listened. The buzz was gone. But another Post-it said it was time to empty the vacuum. I unlatched the canister, took the bag out to the garden, and ripped it open. I stood back as the dust clouded up. I tore a tall flower from the ground and used the stem to stir around the contents. Fly carcasses dotted the dust balls and bits of glass. Tangled in the mess was a silver chain that made my stomach turn over. It was Mom's anklet, the one she always wore. I lifted it with the stem and carried it inside. After I rinsed it off, I stretched it out on the counter and looked at the letters of her name: S-E-R-E-N-A.

Downing a bowl of cereal, I tried to ignore the glinting silver on the counter. I laid a napkin over it, poured some more coffee, and studied the lump while I ate.

Even through the napkin I could feel the heat of the silver anklet and see the outline of the nameplate. I should get rid of it, but it was Mom's favorite piece of jewelry. She wore it every day. With the napkin still over it, I grabbed it and stuck it in an outside pocket in my backpack. I'd send it to her when she finally let me know where she was.

I took a few baskets from the pile by the shop and loaded them into the back of the car. I filled up the gas tank at the convenience store and bought two coffees—one for me and one for Liz—and drove to the MacPhees' house.

In the kitchen, Marty was sneaking an apple into Liz's backpack. "Your hair is adorable!" Mrs. MacPhee said. "By the way, I've been meaning to ask you if you need a blow-dryer. I happen to have one too many!" She pointed behind her, toward her bathroom.

"All set, but thank you. The baskets are in the back of the car."

Marty flew by me. "Oh, thank your mother for me. She has such a creative knack. A gift. She should do something with it." She looked back. "I mean something more—go big, I mean. It's a crime—"

I'd stopped listening and went to Liz's room.

"What did you do to yourself!" Liz said. She shivered and said, "Let's go. We can fix it in the car." She pointed me down the hall.

"I like it," I said, opening the front door. "It's the new me."

"No, it's not. It's your mother," she said, walking down the path. "And I can't believe you're driving her car around. Won't she be pissed?" Liz said.

"She won't even know."

Marty came toward us with a basket of dried flowers on either arm. "Bye, hun," she said.

"Bye, Mom," Liz said, kissing the lavender-scented air.

I got in and buckled my seat belt.

"Here," she said, handing me two hair clips.

I looked in the rearview mirror. "What?"

"Let me do it," she said, turning my chin toward her. She pinned my new bangs back and nodded satisfactorily.

I didn't bother to look, just handed her the coffee.

"Thanks, Claude."

"You want to go to the mall after school?" I asked, sipping as I drove. I'd been trying to plan something fun and spontaneous since I'd skipped the big party at Jenna's house.

"I can't today, but maybe tomorrow after we get our tests back," Liz said. "Quiz me, okay?"

"What test?"

"You're joking. Poetry, Claude—we only have one class together. This is the test. Today. We had the quiz the other day."

"Oh, yeah. Just haven't had my coffee yet." I went through my mental list of lists and didn't see the one that said *Test Tuesday*. But then I remembered what Mr. Springer had said at the end of class. Of course, the test. It would be okay—I loved tests.

Liz and I batted definitions back and forth on the way, practicing until they became automatic. Then we quizzed each other on the bios of the poets we had studied.

The bios I wrote came quickly, and the definitions were a snap. It felt good to have the right answers in the right spaces. There was no other feeling like it. It was something I could count on. If I studied hard and put down the right answers, I got an A+.

I put my pencil down with a satisfying slap and began a

doodle on the back of the paper while the rest of the class finished up.

Someone's eyes were on me. I looked up, and Mr. Springer gave me a smile and a nod. He took a pencil from the pottery jar on his desk and wrote something down. I bit the inside of my cheek. The bell rang, and everyone pushed their way out, dropping their tests on his desk in a sloppy pile. When I got there, I straightened it out, holding up the line in the process. Voices urged me on, reminding me that it was the end of school, telling me to get a life. When I turned, I could see that Mr. Springer and Liz were sharing a look.

"What?" I said. I laughed a little. "It's a mess."

Mr. Springer turned back to Liz and said something, smiling. I stepped aside and let the line out the door as Ms. Frost popped in with her gray braids and yellow pencils.

"Claudine?" she said. "Are you going down to see your mom this weekend?"

"This weekend?" I looked for nothing in particular in my backpack. "Maybe next weekend."

"This would be the only Family Weekend. Did you call to make a reservation?" She came over to me.

When I only shrugged, she said, "Claudine, I'm worried about you being alone. Twenty-eight days is a long time to be without your mom. It's only been a little over a week, and I have a feeling you miss her already."

I swallowed, and my eyes filled while I rearranged some folders and books in my backpack like something was missing. I put my hand into a small zipper pocket and felt the familiar silver chain and put it into the pocket of my jeans.

"I'm right, aren't I?" she said. I felt her arm around me. "Stop by my office and we can talk about it, okay?"

I hoisted my backpack on my shoulder. "I'm fine, really. Liz and"—I motioned at the door—"the MacPhees are there for me."

Ms. Frost nodded. "So you'll check in with them?" she said.

"Yup," I said, moving closer to the door.

Liz appeared at my side. "Ready to go?" she said.

When we were out the double doors, she stopped me. "I heard that. Claude, are you sure you're okay without your mom home?"

"I'm fine. I love it, Liz." I punched the air.

"Whoa," she said, ducking.

"I can eat when I want, watch what I want on TV, play music as loud as I want. I don't have to worry about any-one calling to tell me Mom's been in an accident or passed out in someone's house." I could feel the heat in my cheeks and knew they were red because everyone knew what I said was true. That Mom had done all those things.

Dear Mom,

Today I aced another test. I wish you showed some enthusiasm. You just roll your eyes and shake your head like it's some trick. It's just hard work, Mom. You could do it, too. It's not too late still. Go back and graduate.

I'll help you. There I go again. Always trying to help and fix and control and improve.

It's kind of like all those times I had you on the program. I sent you to meetings, I gave you books, I smelled your breath, I buried your beer in the backyard.

—Claude

mall
today

help Liz with
health report

feed
Moonpie

give away
old clothes

shower and
start wash

get
taillight

wash floor
in bathroom

10

ON THE WAY TO POETRY, I walked by the Staff
Lounge and saw Ms. Frost and Mr. Springer going
over some papers at a table near the coffee station. Mr.
Springer pushed his glasses up on his nose and nodded
gravely. Ms. Frost shook her head. I stood in the doorway and craned my neck to see the paper. No name, but I
could tell it was one of Mr. Springer's tests.

They looked up.

"Claudine," Ms. Frost said. She motioned for me to wait,
but I was gone before she was out the door.

I waited until the class was filled, then I took my seat
just as Mr. Springer flipped the test over on my desk. "Let's
talk," he said.

I lifted the edge enough to see some red writing, and a question mark.

Jenna stood and yelled from across the room. "Claude, my first A ever!"

I smiled and slid my test into my backpack.

Mr. Springer flipped off the lights and started a video documentary called *Walking in a Writer's World*. We were supposed to take notes about how place has meaning in each writer's work. I couldn't make sense of it. The sea, the mountains, whatever. I slid my notebook from my backpack and worked on my list by the light of the TV screen. The flashes of light played over the string of ideas for ordering my life. I had school; I had my friends; I had home. Home had the biggest list. From bathroom to outside work, there were at least twenty-five items. As I arranged them, a shadow darkened the page and I saw that Mr. Springer was at my side. I shut my notebook and looked up, but his eyes were on the screen. A woman was walking along the beach. The wind blew her hair and skirt, so that it looked like work just to walk. "The way I work is I wait until the poem writes itself. It stays inside me and I work on it when I walk, when I cook, whenever, and then one day it just has to be written. It's born. See?"

No, I didn't see. I could tell by the snorts that a few others didn't either, but they were the regular slackers. With a flash I remembered that I loved the poet in the film; I used to read her. Last year I would have been all over this assignment. What was happening to me?

The lights came on, and everyone began to talk at once.

I let myself be carried out with the crowd, avoiding Mr. Springer and forcing myself to resist the urge to neaten the rows of desks. They'll just get messy again; they'll just get messy again. Instead I counted them.

Liz was waiting at my car. "Hey, what'd you get?" she said. "I got an A. An A!"

"Great," I said. My skin felt itchy. It was because I hadn't gone back to straighten the desks. I picked at the tenderest spots on my fingers and thumbs.

"Can I have a ride to group?" She checked me out and straightened my hair.

I looked like shit, I guessed. "Where's your car?"

"Dad wants to take it in for a safety tune-up."

"What a guy," I said, getting in. "Come on."

"Are you mad at him?"

"I guess I am. I'm not sure why, though." We both laughed a little.

"First group, and then we're going to pick up Jenna and go to the mall, right?" Liz said.

"Right," I said. "So, how's it going on the report? Need any help?"

"I'm doing okay. You gave me a great start. I think I've got it under control now," Liz said.

I tapped out a rhythm on the steering wheel, alternating thumbs. *One, two, three, four, five, one, two, three, four, five, one, two, three, four, five.*

Liz clicked on the radio.

I beat the wheel harder.

"What did you get?" she asked.

"What do you mean?"

"On your test," she said.

"What do you think?"

She laughed. "Yeah, pretty easy," she said. "We probably could have skipped the studying."

"Probably."

"Is everybody here?" Lydia looked around. "I think it's important to begin on time." She was talking about Matt. I knew he was still at school, in the main office. I'd heard him on the phone arguing with his dad, but I didn't tell her. "If nobody has anything, let's talk about—"

"I have something," I said. All heads turned to me.

"I wanted to share about a book I've read. It's called *The Daily New*. Get it? It's a play on *The Daily News*. Anyway—" I said.

Deb sighed loudly.

"Anyway," I said, "every day has a new affirmation to think about. Like: 'I can be proud of the choices I make,' or 'I will enjoy myself today and be spontaneous,' or 'I am not alone.'"

"I'd like to borrow that," Liz said.

"I have a couple of those that Mom and Dad have given me," Willa said. "And Dad has one for alcoholics."

Willa continued, "Today my morning affirmation said something about letting other people take care of themselves, and at the bottom of the page was the daily Think

About: Recall a time when you involved yourself with someone's recovery process. Negatively or positively."

"I think I have that book. I guess I didn't read it today, and I never do the Think Abouts anyway," Hanna said.

Lydia was enjoying the activity in the group. Her eyes moved from one to another. I wasn't. I wanted to steer the conversation in a different direction. I hated when it got chaotic like this, with everyone jumping in at once.

Matt came in and sat down. "What's up?"

"Say it again, Willa," Lydia said.

Deb sighed again. Maybe she felt the same way I did.

"Recall a time when you involved yourself with someone's recovery process. Negatively or positively," Willa said.

"This is like truth or dare," Deb said.

"I got one," Blake said.

When Blake talked, it was so slow and quiet. I prepared myself for sleep.

"I was always scared of my mother when she drank, so I left the room." He folded his pasty arms across his belly. I took note of the smoothness of his skin, that he had no stubble. He was Matt's polar opposite. "I left the house, too. Especially when she was loud."

The group waited. Feet shuffled, and Matt drummed softly on his knees.

Blake said, "That was my involvement. I guess it was no involvement."

He reminded me of a fish near death, only the lips

moved as he gasped for a breath. I would call him Blank from now on. He looked dead in the eyes. I'd call him Blank. Blank.

"I guess that's a negative. I should've said something."

"It's never too late, Blake," Hanna said.

He looked at her, unmoving. What did she know? Sometimes it is too late.

A silence weighed heavy in the room. I took advantage of the quiet. "There are lots of positive ways to get involved," I said.

"Do tell," Matt said.

I ignored him. "You can buy them a book or a tape. You can suggest nutritious snacks and do active things instead of sitting around in a dark, smoky house. You can encourage each step they take and be there for them if they mess up—ready to forgive. You can make sure they know you love them no matter what. You can—"

"Take a break, Claude," Matt said. "How is that positive? You gave him a load of codependent shit to do when it's pretty clear that he and his mother are a fucked-up mess." He looked to Lydia and shrugged an oops. "Sorry," he said.

"Matt, I didn't mean to do them all at once. It's just a list of ways to bring some positivity into the relationship," I said.

Willa nodded. "Positivity. She's right; we all need it. Especially me."

"Oh, yeah, never enough these days," Chris said.

"It's mostly crap, and you know it," Matt said. He leaned out to look at me. His curls hung down to his eyes, and even though he was glaring at me, I didn't care. "You do know that it's the *drunk's* job to get it together, right?"

I had to look away from his eyes. Especially because I thought he might be a little bit right.

Jenna was at Mother's Beach with the usual crowd that hung there.

She skipped over and got in, handing a pot of lip gloss into the front. "Try this," she said. "Peach Blossom."

I could smell the sickly sweetness of it, and I gagged quietly. Liz stuck her finger in it and smeared it over her lips.

Jenna stuck the pot under my nose. "No thanks, I've got my own." I reached into the glove compartment and put my own color on. I checked myself before we backed out. Just right.

"That's your color, Claude," she said.

"I know." Actually it was Mom's, but it worked on me.

The mall was exactly what I wanted: the three of us acting like kids in a commercial. We were laughing, happy teens. Giddiness was a strange feeling, sort of like being tickled. I loved it and dove right into the part, following where Liz and Jenna went and laughing at the things they laughed at. We put on headphones at the music store and danced in the aisles.

And then I saw Mom's favorite store, Deja's. A gauzy Indian-print shirt hung outside the store. Her favorite song played inside. I took down the shirt and followed the sound of the Grateful Dead into the cramped room.

"Can I try it on?" I asked, holding it up for the clerk to see.

"Oh, Claude, come on," Liz said. "This isn't you; you're jeans and a T-shirt, khakis and a polo. What else, Jenna?"

"She's a ponytail." She put her hands on her hips.

I went into a dressing room anyway. The smell of vanilla musk oil and the light touch of the material was like a kiss from Mom. I held the shirt to my face and breathed. Tears pooled behind my lids, but I blinked them back. "Mom," I whispered.

A pair of hip-huggers with a fringe belt appeared over the top of the door, and Liz said, "You might as well go all the way."

"Thanks," I said. I stepped out of my own pants, pulled up the hip-huggers, and tied up the belt. When I picked up my pants, a silver anklet fell in a knot at my feet. Mom's anklet.

"What was that?" Jenna asked.

"I'll be right there," I said. I fastened it around my ankle, the opposite foot from the one with the toe ring, and stepped back to take in my reflection. "Excellent." I pulled the curtain back and stepped out.

Liz and Jenna went white and looked at each other. Their mouths opened and then closed. "It's too creepy," Liz said.

"What's wrong?" I said, smoothing the shirt. "Everything fits perfectly."

"Too perfect," Jenna said.

"Yeah, you look exactly like your mom, Claudine. Exactly."

I went into the dressing room again and looked. I felt right and serene. "I'll get it all," I called out. "And I'll wear it now."

While I paid, Liz and Jenna waited outside the store. We were supposed to be seeing a movie, but it had already started.

"Let's get going," I said.

"No, wait," Jenna said. "The movie. We haven't missed that much."

Liz nodded.

"I've got stuff to do still," I said. "And school tomorrow."

"Who are you, Cinderella?" Jenna asked.

"Come on, Claude," Liz said. She did her sad face for me.

"I'm beat," I said, and began walking. They stayed a few steps behind me, heads together, whispering.

We drove in silence, except for Jenna's chatter to Liz and Liz's grunts back. As I passed the sign for Deep Cove, my stomach began to tighten and I felt the anklet heavy around my ankle.

After I dropped them off at Liz's house, I drove to the beach and parked at the seawall. The air was thick with salt and cooler than it had been during the day, but I left my sweatshirt in the car. Waves slapped the shore at half tide. I stood on top of the cement block wall, shook my hair out, and spread my arms wide, letting the breeze touch me. Gauzy waves of Indian print rippled against my skin, making me smile. Strange, I thought, I'd always hated this look.

Dear Mom,

It's the middle of the night, and I woke up on my hands and knees on the bathroom floor! I don't remember getting there, but when I woke up, I was reaching out behind the toilet. Gross, huh? I got the broom and swept back there, and you know what I found? A necklace of yours. It was the blue stone dragonfly necklace on the leather thong. I put it on and it goes perfectly with the outfit I bought at Deja's. I think of you whenever I look at the shirt. You'd love it.

Now I'm awake and I can't sleep. I think I'll bag up all my ugly clothes and take them to a Goodwill.

—Claude

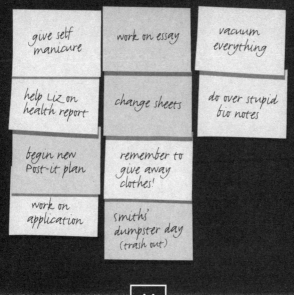

give self
manicure

work on essay

vacuum
everything

help Liz on
health report

change sheets

do over stupid
bio notes

begin new
Post-it plan

remember to
give away
clothes!

work on
application

smiths'
dumpster day
(trash out)

11

L IZ STARED AT ME DURING POETRY CLASS. When I
looked back, she looked away. If she was mad about
not going to the movie, she didn't say. I moved my chair
over and wrote a list of chores I needed to do and covered
it with my hand. There was actual dirt on my sheets, and I
had to change them. I mean, that was disgusting. Moonpie
had brought in half the garden.

"It's good to see someone taking notes," said Mr.
Springer. "It's not a bad idea to write something down if it
resonates with you."

I looked down at the list of household chores and giggled.

A pencil poked me in the back. "Brownnoser," Matt
said.

I wrote Liz a note and slid it over to her. *Let's meet in the library after school to work on your health report. I have some ideas for you. C.*

"Claudine, anything you'd like to share?" Mr. Springer asked.

"No, it's personal," I said, turning the page of the notebook.

Mr. Springer began passing out yellow three-by-three Post-it pads. "Take the packet I made for you of American poets and the Post-its." He moved to the board, where he'd written the title FIGURATIVE SPEECH. Below were columns for metaphor, simile, alliteration, onomatopoeia, etc. "Find examples of these in the poetry. Copy them with the author and name of the poem on the back and put your own name on the front. Stick them in the appropriate column, your name out."

The class moved as one mass up to the board. Packet pages flipped frantically and pencils scribbled as they competed to fill the columns. Above their heads I could only see the tops of the columns. With a blast of clarity that only happens when I'm very focused, I saw what I needed to do. I sucked in my breath with a loud, "Oh!" and heads turned to see me staring at the wall graph. Instead of figurative language, I saw my life laid out on the board. Monday, Tuesday, Wednesday, etc. Below each day I would list the daily chores.

"A revelation?" Mr. Springer said.

"Maybe," I said.

The idea was huge. I'd use different-colored Post-its for

different days of the week. Each chore would have its own sticky note, and I'd put them on the cupboards in vertical columns so I could follow my daily progress. This idea was going to make an incredible change in my whole life. I could even designate another color for long-term projects like home repairs, winterizing, spring cleaning. This was doable. It would fix everything. I would have clean hair every day, my lunch would be packed, and the cat would be fed. I would even coordinate my grocery list with a menu plan.

Why hadn't I thought of this earlier? If Mom and I had used an organizing tool like this when I was growing up, I wouldn't have scrambled every morning to clean up and make sure she was awake and eating. I would have remembered to check the fridge for beer and dump it out before school instead of later, in the middle of a party when she was already smashed. I would have been able to make the bus on time and been focused in class instead of worrying if Mom had gotten up that day. A Post-it system would have given her a structure to follow every day and one for me, too. A wave of despair overtook me, and I began to sob uncontrollably. I turned my back on the class and forced myself to breathe the dark panic away.

The slapping shut of notebooks and moving of chairs brought me back to the room. I wiped my nose and sat down to pack my books. Mr. Springer handed me some papers.

"Thanks," I said, glad to have something more to do.

He waited beside my desk.

"Those were the wrong notes, Claudine. You must have meant them for something else." He handed me the letter I'd written to Mom about stealing things from the MacPhees.

My heart thudded in my chest and my cheeks burned as I ran through my lists. *How'd this even get out of my binder?* "It's personal. I thought I mailed it."

"Maybe you mailed the biography notes to your mom." He looked down at me and waited. "It's okay, Claudine. I didn't read it." The classroom was clearing, and I felt the familiar panic rise in my throat as I tried to remember the notes and passing the letter in to him. He was right—I must have mailed it to Mom. I searched for something to hand him. "Here. No, that's not it." I dug deeper. "It's buried under here somewhere, I'm sure. Shoot." I shrugged. "Sorry."

"You don't have the assignment?"

"It must be in the mail. Someone at Jackson Heights is reading something very interesting." I smiled like it was some sort of funny mix-up.

"Pass it in by Monday."

Frantic fists pounded inside my chest. This was my best subject, and I was messing up.

"I'll have it for you. Don't worry."

"Frankly, I am a little worried, Claudine. You aren't yourself, and I know why."

I didn't look at him. I kept my eyes on the floor.

"You look exhausted, and I know you must be worried about your mother. A lot of people understand what you're going through. You're not alone."

Ah, the magic words. Code words. *He's one of us. Oooo. Maybe there's a special handshake, too.* The recovery process had seemed the thing to do when I needed to help Mom, but now I wasn't so sure. At least not when it involved me.

He walked out the door and down the hall with me.

My plodding feet and racing heart were out of sync. I breathed through my nose and willed my heart to slow as he walked beside me. Kids poured from classrooms and rushed to get to their lockers.

"Let's go talk to Ms. Frost."

"No. I'm fine. I have an appointment with her later—about the scholarship."

"Oh, the scholarship. Congratulations on your nomination." He smiled and clamped his hand on my shoulder. "She's a good listener, too. Can I write you a hall pass?"

We were standing in front of her closed door.

Watch everyone putting their books away, I told myself. *See the guys fooling around at their lockers? Keep your eyes on them. Focus. Hear the coach chewing out his quarterback? Focus on this moment and breathe. Go through your list: Did you take out the trash? No. Did you feed Moonpie? Yes.* If I'd thought of the Post-it Plan earlier, this never would have happened. I would've had everything under control.

"Claudine, I care about you and your future. Let me know if you feel overloaded."

I gave him a quick smile and said, "I have to do some work at the library."

He nodded. And I left him in the hall.

The school library had a chair in a back corner beside a window that looked out onto the field where girls were practicing field hockey. Sports seemed like such a waste of time when there were so many important things to finish. At the same time, a miniature of myself, one deep inside, wanted to see what it would be like to be one of the normals. I'd be a good runner if I ever tried. I had "legs up to here," people always said. I brushed that image away as I whipped out my list. Liz was at the top of the list and she was late. I might have to cross her off.

The double doors opened, and I looked up at the sound. Liz, with Jenna close behind, came in, giggling. They went to the librarian and whispered something, and then left, muffling their laughter in the rush. *That was me last week,* I thought. List tight in my fist, I rushed after them, but they were gone when I reached the hall.

Mr. MacPhee was on both knees, planting bulbs along his brick path. He waved me over.

"Hey-hey, Claude!" he called.

"Is Liz here?"

"She went to the movies with Jenna Carver, the one they missed last night," he said, resting an arm on one knee.

My mouth went dry. She didn't tell me that. They left without asking me.

I barely heard Mr. MacPhee talking to me. He took a step forward. "How about taking this one for your mother's garden? I'm beat. I can't do another thing."

I don't think Mom had ever owned such a huge bulb.

But there it was again, another MacPhee hand-me-down. "No thanks, it's a little early for bulbs," I said.

"So Liz tells me that your mother is still at Jackson Heights?" He set the bulb down and dug a hole for it.

"Yup, still there," I said. I started to walk away.

"I'm looking into Jackson Heights, too."

I turned around. I didn't know where to go with this.

He picked the bulb up and handed it to me. "Your mother's doing the right thing. This could be a coming-home gift."

I took the lumpy bulb. It was heavy for what it looked like. I smiled and said, "Thank you."

When Liz and Jenna came out of the theater, I was standing where they'd bump into me.

"Hi, how's it going?"

Their mouths opened and they looked at each other.

"What's wrong?" I asked. "Surprised?"

Jenna began, "You missed it again."

Liz said, "Man, Claude, you didn't show up, so—"

"So you went without me. And now I'm going to see it."

They said nothing.

"I would've come today, you know," I squeezed between them and bought my ticket. I didn't look back.

Hunkering down in my seat, I sat in the darkened theater with my hands tucked into my sleeves and shivered. The place was a germ factory. The movie was stupid. A girl and a guy get caught on an island. What will they do until they get rescued? Duh.

I left before they were rescued and drove home with the bulb from Mr. MacPhee on the seat beside me. I reached for an antibacterial wipe from the glove compartment and wiped my hands while I steered with my elbows. Then I wiped down the steering wheel, the bulb, and the seat. Everything was better already.

Moonpie was waiting on the steps, and Linwood was parked in front of the trailer. He hopped out of his truck and came toward the car. His smile turned into a glare when I looked up at him.

"What the hell, girl?"

"What?"

"Your mother know you got her stuff? Her car?"

"Yeah," I said, fiddling with the keys.

He motioned to the door. "Locking the door now?"

"I lock it when I leave," I said, turning the key. "That's what normal people do."

"Serena never locks it," he said, following me in.

"I rest my case."

I put my backpack on the counter and frowned when he set a six-pack down beside it.

"She's not here, Linwood."

He whipped off his sweatshirt, and the odor of baitfish wafted up. I took a step back.

"What's all this?" he asked, motioning to the Post-its with an unopened beer.

"Reminders," I said. I thought of my new idea and the colorful columns that I'd make.

"Reminders for what?"

"For my life, what do you think?"

His beer hissed open, and it all came rushing back in a nauseating second. How much I hated him, how he had sabotaged Mom's recoveries. How she'd let him come back every time they broke up.

It was pretty simple: when Linwood was around, Mom drank more; when Linwood was gone, Mom drank less.

"Linwood, you could use a few reminders yourself, like: 'Get a life' or 'Be nice,'" I said. "Or, 'Take a shower, you smell like a bait barrel.'" I crossed my arms over my chest.

He chuckled to himself. "You're cold, girl, cold as your mother is, but I like you anyways. And you look good in her clothes." He jutted his chin out at me. "And her jewelry, too. Looks good."

"You pig."

He took a haul off his beer and slammed it on the counter. "I can't believe she didn't say nothin' to me. It ain't like her."

"Get out, Linwood, and take your nasty-smelling sweatshirt with you." I moved toward the beer, but he scooped it up.

His lips turned down. "I thought she'd at least call." He stood up. "Tell me where she's at," he said. He took a giant step forward. "I'm gonna go see her."

"No!" The smell of beer was making me sway, bringing nausea with it. The image of Mom white-faced, a drained beer bottle beside her, appeared in my mind. "Get out!" I screamed.

"Jeezus! Okay, okay, I'm outta here." He grabbed his sweatshirt and six-pack.

I ran for the bathroom and retched in the toilet bowl.

When I stood again and faced myself in the mirror, it was my mother's face I saw. This was her after a rough night—gray, shaky, scraggle-haired. I couldn't shut my eyes to this. I turned on the shower and undressed. I was disgusting again. I let the spray prick my skin with hot beads of water while I kneaded the puff into a lavender-scented lather. It'll be okay in a minute, I thought. I used the nailbrush on my fingertips, but it took more than a few minutes to get off the dirt from the day. It was a day where so much had changed. Liz had changed, and Linwood wouldn't stay away. Even Mr. Springer was different. It would take a long time to make this day clean.

I sat in front of the silent television and wrote Mom a letter.

Dear Mom,

I have a great idea. It's so great that you need to know about it before you come back. It'll make life sooooo much easier. You can come home and slide right into your new routine. I know how hard you're working in your recovery. You should be supported.

That's what's missing from the whole recovery process: support.

So, here's the plan: Today in poetry class I got the idea to use Post-its to help us keep a schedule. Every day of the week will have a color code and a list of five to ten jobs that need to get done. Because Post-its are so cool (easy to stick and remove), we can easily add and take away jobs. I'll be posting them on the cupboard doors. Each cupboard gets a day. It'll be right here in front of us.

The only thing is that I wish we'd been this organized before you left. I never thought of anything like this before, when we needed it most. I'm sorry, Mom. I'll make it work this time!

—Claude

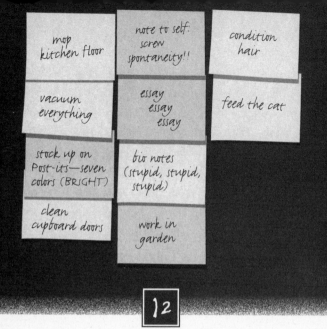

mop
kitchen floor

note to self:
screw
spontaneity!!

condition
hair

vacuum
everything

essay
essay
essay

feed the cat

stock up on
Post-its—seven
colors (BRIGHT)

bio notes
(stupid, stupid,
stupid)

clean
cupboard doors

work in
garden

12

Liz had Art Club on Fridays. I sat in the basement rooms where art classes were held, waiting for her perched on a long table covered in splotches of paint and glue. I didn't know what she wanted, but she'd passed me a note in poetry class that said to meet her after school. Maybe it was more help with health. I should have insisted on helping her finish when I had more time.

Liz came into the room holding a mobile with cloth people dangling from strings.

"I wanted to show you this and talk to you about something," she said, stepping momentarily on a chair to hang it from a pipe.

"Excellent job," I said, and I meant it.

A family hung from the driftwood mobile, and each person was unique. Liz had sewn clothing and hair for each one. Even the expressions were hand sewn.

"This one is the Scapegoat. Can you tell? He pierced everything and has a tattoo on his butt." She pulled down his pants and showed a heart with an arrow through it. "He's out to shake things up."

"This is really good, Liz. I can tell you've learned a lot."

"Thanks to you," she said, bumping me. "Check this out." She held up a girl with blond hair and light pink everything. "She's almost see-through because I want her to be the Adjuster. She doesn't make waves; she'll adjust to whatever happens. Maybe I should have made her out of clay."

"No, this is great, Liz."

"And this one is the Responsible One." She spun her around. Long brown hair in a clip, jeans, T-shirt, a pencil and list in one hand and a broom in the other.

I stared at the mini-me.

She touched my arm, and I flinched.

"Don't be mad."

I kept my eyes on the spinning girl with the list.

"I told the librarian to tell you to meet us at the movie. We were going to be late for it. She said you ran out before she could stop you."

I didn't move or look up.

She hopped up on the table beside me. "Claude, you're a mess. You need to talk to someone."

I moved away and looked out the basement window. I

could see people getting into cars and a corner of the track where the cross-country team was gathered.

"You've helped me so much, Claude. I never would've started group, or understood the roles we play when someone we love is addicted, if you hadn't helped me to understand." She put her hand on my back. "I never would've gotten this report done without your support. You taught me a lot, Claude."

So she was all done with the health report.

"But I know from everything I've learned that you need help. You're deeply codependent."

"Oh, please!" I said, jumping down.

"You're codependent and something else. Look at your hands! They're practically bleeding from all the washing and picking you do. And you take so many showers that your hair is going to fall out." She put on the confused-pity look and stepped closer. "You've always been a little obsessive-compulsive. It was kind of funny. Remember? But now—"

"What?" I put my hand to my head and felt the crispy ends.

"You're out of control. Claude, you haven't changed your clothes since you bought them." She shook her head disapprovingly. "That's so not you."

I looked up at the mobile that had finally stopped moving and ripped the Responsible One off and whipped her across the room.

At group I sat on the other side, away from Liz. Today it wasn't hard to be out of my regular seat. Everything looked different from the other side, and I liked it. I could see the kitchen where the potluck casseroles were heated up, the piano room where I'd banged on the keys and got in trouble, and the corner where they put a wingback chair for Santa Claus. When I was seven, my wish for Christmas had been to have a father. I was sure that's what Mom needed. Soon she had Linwood.

Matt sat with his elbows on his knees and his eyes on some invisible spot on the floor. He looked like he might punch out someone if they got too close. Chris and Deb talked quietly, looking over at him every once in a while. *Something's up with him,* I thought. Willa and Hanna were passing out clipboards, and Liz and Lydia were talking. The whole place had the feeling of a funeral home.

Blake sat down next to me.

"Who died?" I said to him.

"Matt's dad. He drove into a stone wall."

I saw Matt look away. He'd heard me. I'm an idiot.

"I'm sorry, Matt," I said, knowing it was a ridiculous thing to say, and not even a little helpful.

Lydia set her coffee on the table behind her and stood up. "Well, Matt's asked that . . ." She shook her head and gestured to Matt with her hand. "Matt, please tell the group what you told me. I think you can speak on this better than I can." She sat back down and quickly reached for her cup.

"My dad's dead." He kept his eyes on the floor. "I don't want to talk about it, so I'll keep it simple for now. He was drunk when he died. He drove the car into the big stone wall on O'Henry Corner. I mean, who wouldn't see that comin'? I don't know. Today I can't really talk about it, but I will sometime, and I can't believe I'm saying this, but I'm glad you'll all be here to listen when I'm ready." He pinched the bridge of his nose and swallowed hard. My own eyes stung, and others cried openly.

For some minutes it was quiet except for a few sniffs and shifting feet. I wanted Chris to move so I could sit next to Matt and tell him that the aching, empty hole he felt inside was normal, that it stays with you day and night, and that after a while it becomes a part of you and you kind of befriend it. I wanted to ask him if he had nightmares and memories that swept him away from real life. I wanted to suggest that he write his dad a letter.

"Matt," Blake said, "I think I need to go."

Everyone looked at Blake like he was some kind of heartless monster. But Matt said, "No problem, man. This is probably a bad time to talk."

"It's just that this has me thinking I ought to talk to my parents," Blake said.

"It's whatever you guys think," Lydia said. "We can finish early today unless anyone wants to talk."

"Yeah, maybe I should go, too," Chris said. "Can I give anyone a ride?"

"Me, please," Deb said, getting up.

Soon the room was cleared except for Liz, Lydia, Matt, and me.

I walked toward his chair and stood there, not knowing what to say.

He leaned back so I could see his eyes. Tears and pain.

In my head I was thinking, *Anytime you want to talk, Matt.* But what came out was a sigh and, "It sucks, doesn't it?"

"Jeez, Claude," Liz said. I heard her walk out the door with Lydia.

Matt nodded and stood up. I could smell his sweat. "You got that right."

"You need a ride?" I said.

"No, I'm going to the beach."

We walked down the steps. "It's not what you expected, is it?" I said.

"No, I still keep thinking he's going to be at home in the chair."

"Call me if you want to talk."

"Thanks, Claude," he said, giving my arm a soft punch.

I bought ten packs of three-by-three fluorescent notes— everything they had in bright colors. At the last minute, I grabbed a large-size Post-it pad with blue-green lines. That would be for things to do that weren't daily jobs: the long-term projects. I saw myself getting up on time and checking in with a morning list, being ready for each day and going out the door prepared for whatever would come my way. Every time Liz came into my head, I let her fly back out. I never thought of her for more than a second. I stayed on task.

In the kitchen, I designated each day with one color and made columns of squares on each cupboard door. I wrote the daily chores on each of them and gave each day a special job, like Laundry Day, Change the Sheets Day, Shopping Day, and Extra Chore Day. And, of course, every day could use a little vacuuming.

Dear Mom,

It was such a bad day. But the Post-it plan looks good. That's all that's good, though. Our life will be orderly now, but something's changed with Liz. She's acting different. She's calling me codependent and telling me I'm weird. She thinks she knows everything now. I feel strange, like I'm lost in my own world, but my world is changed and it changed without telling me.

Once, you and Candy had a major fight, remember? But you guys made up the next day, and she said something like, "Everyone's an asshole sometimes. Let's forget it." I don't know if this is the same thing. Liz looks at me like she doesn't know me.

And Matt's dad was killed when he drove drunk. I didn't know him, but I know Matt and I see his pain, and I know you and it makes me feel shaky. I have that dark, heavy feeling in my bones again.

I'm scared for you when you're not with me.

—Claude

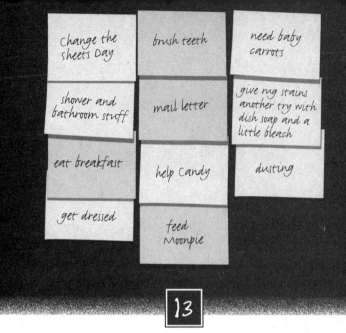

change the
sheets Day

brush teeth

need baby
carrots

shower and
bathroom stuff

mail letter

give rug stains
another try with
dish soap and a
little bleach

eat breakfast

help Candy

dusting

get dressed

feed
Moonpie

13

Saturday CHANGE THE SHEETS DAY

I HOPPED OUT OF BED and ran to the kitchen to see
the bright blue vertical column that designated
Saturday on the cupboard door.

This will be so much easier, I thought as I sat at the
kitchen table with my coffee and granola. I looked around
in satisfaction. I was doing it: keeping a well-ordered,
clean, and cheerful house.

The phone rang while I was in the middle of washing
the coffee pot.

"Is she back?"

"Candy?"

"No, Shania Twain." She broke into song.

I groaned at her poor imitation and said, "Sorry, Candy."

Candy waited.

"Nope."

"I need help this weekend."

"You can count on me. I just have to do a couple of things around here, but—"

"Either you're working, or you're not. Which is it?"

"I'll be there."

The stain by the kitchen door had spread to a watery rust color, and even though most of it was under the rug, the edges of the stain peeked out and reminded me every day. I lifted the corner and sprayed rug cleaner without looking, then scrubbed up the lather. *I'll vacuum it later,* I thought.

The Saturday chores were done, and now I had to rake up the mess I'd made with the vacuum bag; also, the flower beds were a wreck. They needed major weeding and thinning out.

On my hands and knees, I moved the catnip Moonpie had destroyed and thinned the marjoram. Fall was the time that Mom transplanted a lot of her beds. She said she liked to do it then instead of during the spring because the plants were up and she could see what she was doing. Beside the catnip was a needy-looking purple flower I didn't know. The clusters drooped anemically. The silver artemisia needed to be reined in, and the thyme was spreading out of control.

There was so much to do. How could she leave these plants here? How could she leave me?

When I walked back into the trailer from the garden, I found two things: the red message light blinking and a mound of cat poop on the rug, not far from where Liz had spilled her soda. Beads of sweat formed on my forehead. How did that happen? Before I did anything, I washed off the garden soil. I used the vegetable brush with concentrated dish soap. Running the water as hot as I could stand it, I scrubbed deep in the cracks of my skin to get the soil out. I felt a bristle pierce my index finger, and a dot of blood grew. I rinsed it off and brushed again and again until I felt more and more sharp pains and more dots of blood appeared.

"No," I said, panting over the sink as I washed. "Stop it! Stop it, now! It hurts! Why can't I stop? Make me stop!"

Moonpie yowled to go out.

"Goddamn cat!" I pushed off the faucets without drying my hands and chased him around the trailer until he scrambled under Mom's bed.

"Shit!" I said, lying back on the bed. "You pain-in-the-ass cat!" How did I forget to let him out? It was right there on the list. I sat up and stomped my foot on the floor, and he shot out from under the bed and made a beeline for the door.

I washed up again and pushed the blinking red light. "You have one message," said the machine voice. "Ten thirty-five."

"Man, Claudine, you're starting to act just like your mother."

I was late for Candy.

I went to the sink and washed my hands and face again and set to work on Moonpie's stain. The job would be much more involved than Liz's soda stain. No doubt about that.

I drove, listening to the weatherman.

"You can expect a drab and dreary day today," the weatherman said. "Rain starting tonight with Hurricane Gert possibly turning our way. Stayed tuned for the latest updates." I turned the radio off.

It was true what Candy had said about Mom. She'd blown her off many times. It was typical Mom behavior. But if anyone ever forgot her, or was late and didn't call, she would be frantic. Frantic like one of those psycho-dogs that eat the carpet if you leave them alone.

When I came around the beach into Deep Cove, I passed Linwood and his buddies leaning up against Robbie Holt's truck at the boat ramp, laughing. He raised his beer to me and smiled. I looked straight ahead and kept driving until I pulled into the Seaside and parked beside Candy's green Impala.

She was just coming out of the door carrying a pile of dirty linens and heading into the washroom. When she didn't look up, I knew there was trouble. I ran after her. "Candy!"

Her back was to me as she stuffed sheets into the washer. "What? It's a little late."

"I'm sorry. I had a mess at home, and then Mom's garden, too," I said.

She huffed. "Christ, Claude." She shut the lid and cranked the knob.

"I'll go finish up in the rooms," I said.

"There's only one left, and I could do it alone, but since you're here, well, come on."

I followed behind her substantial hips as we climbed to the second-floor rooms. Silently, we each stripped a double bed. I left the sheets in a pile and emptied the garbage cans and collected wrappers and magazines and a *New York Times*.

I heard Candy light a cigarette, and I emptied an ashtray into the garbage and offered it to her.

"Thanks," she said.

I tossed clean sheets onto both of the beds and started in, but she sat and nodded to the other bed for me to sit opposite her.

"What?" I asked.

She waved her arms at the smoke that hung between us. "Claude, I have to tell you something, hun."

My stomach jumped. "What? Tell me what?"

She blew smoke over my shoulder and winced. "Linwood suspects something is up with your mom, so I told him what I think is going on." She took a long drag on her cigarette.

I was frozen; my eyes stayed on her shiny pink lips as they closed around her cigarette. Tell Linwood what? What did she tell Linwood? The ash drooped precariously, and I jumped up, took the ashtray from her hand, and held it under the cigarette. *Tap, tap.*

I ran and opened the window behind her, gulping the damp, salty air and waiting for her to say it.

"Sorry about the smoke. I should know better, huh?" She squashed the butt in the ashtray and tapped out another one from her pack. "Come sit down."

I brushed invisible dust off the mattress pad and sat again.

"I'm sure you know that your mom's been seeing Gary on the side."

I stared out the window at the ocean behind her.

"Well, Linwood suspected something was up, and I had to tell him the truth. That your mom's pulled another disappearing act." She watched my eyes.

I nodded.

"She's taken off to Seattle with him, and I don't think we'll hear from her for a while."

My mind raced back to the morning I woke up and found the mess she'd left. *Mom, why did you start again?*

"Although actually, Claude, in a way it really don't make sense. She usually don't run off without tellin' me all the dirt."

My cheeks grew hot, and my hand went to my chest where my heart was knocking. I took a deep breath and let it out a little at a time to slow the beating down.

"Oh, hun," she said, leaning toward me, "you just hoped she'd gone to rehab." She scooted to the edge of the bed until our knees were touching. "You're a sweet girl, Claude.

You always try to help her, but remember, she's been here before. And she always falls off the wagon and falls in love instead. This ain't nothin' new."

"That's not true anymore. Mom was fine until this happened. She would've stayed recovered if we hadn't screwed up!"

My hands were shaking in my lap. I squeezed them between my knees to stop it, but not before Candy took my wrist.

"Holy shit, girl!" She turned my hand in front of her face, and then she put her cigarette between her lips and took the other wrist. "Mother of god, girl, what happened?" She dropped them and went to the cart. She glared at me as she gathered supplies.

"It's nothing, Candy," I said.

She dumped latex gloves, complimentary hand cream, and Band-Aids on the bed. "You know, I've been working here twenty years and look at my hands." She held them out. They were chubby and tan with long pink nails, unchipped and decked out with a ring on every finger. "I clean all day, I smoke, I drink. But I wear gloves when I scrub."

"I do, too," I whispered.

She took a hand between hers, squirted lotion into it, and massaged each finger. Then she did the same for the other one. A tingle of warmth crept in, and my eyes filled with tears. "Stings like a bastard, don't it? It'll fix you right up, though." She took gauze from the first-aid kit on the cart and wrapped the tips of my thumbs and index fingers and taped them with Band-Aids.

A tear fell on my hand, and she wiped it off with her apron. "Oh, hun, don't cry. I'll come stay with you until we hear from her." She pulled me over to her bed and hugged me hard. "What do you say I keep you company?"

"No," I said. I shook my head against her shoulder. "I mean, no thanks, Candy."

She patted my arm and smoothed my hair.

"Call me whenever, then. Okay?" She stood up and handed me a pair of latex gloves. "Use 'em."

I worked them onto my hands and started back in on the bed.

"Let's make these up together. It'll go a lot faster." She kneed the corner of her bed out and got behind it. She edged the bottom sheet over so I could reach it, and we pulled the elastic corners down on all four sides. I pulled down the edges to smooth out the wrinkles.

"Claude, did your mom ever tell you about the time you were born?"

My hands froze on the bed. I hadn't put Candy and Mom and my birth in the same thought ever, but they had been best friends since Mom moved here in high school.

"Serena was so big with you, and you know how tiny she is. Man, she was as big as a house." She snorted and snapped out another white sheet. It floated down over the bed, hovering for a moment before it settled. "Don't just stand there, girl."

I smoothed out my side and sat down on the opposite bed.

"Claude?"

The numbness that had been running through my veins, keeping me going and pointed in one direction, began to recede, and I felt icy cold. I willed myself to stand up. "I'm just beat, Candy. I have so much homework to make up."

"Oh, well, I remember. That's gotta suck." She threw me a pillow. "Do them up and then you go."

I unfolded the pillowcases and shook out the pillows from their dirty cases.

"Your mom was so freaked when she went into labor. Your grandmother was still in Florida with her boyfriend, and she wasn't okay with the whole baby thing anyway, so I went with your mom to the hospital. She was so scared."

I stuffed a pillow in a case. "The whole baby thing?"

"You."

Mom wouldn't have wanted to be alone. It was weird to think that I hadn't been there to get her through it step by step, picking up the pieces for her, coaching her through labor. I pictured myself with a hospital gown and mask, telling Mom to Breathe! and Push! A laugh escaped.

Candy flicked her lighter. "It ain't funny. Just wait until the day it happens to you."

"It's not going to *happen* to me. Maybe I'll choose it. Maybe I won't."

"Well, anyway, she hadn't gone to one labor class. Not one. In fact, she didn't tell the guy she was knocked up until the day he was packing to move out of town. And, as you know, he never came back neither."

"Candy—" I placed the pillow on the bed and picked it back up.

"And, you know, I didn't know she was pregnant until she started to show, and then she wouldn't even admit it right off." She snorted. "She kept saying she was eating too much, had a flu, filling out."

I held the pillow tightly against my chest.

"She was so scared. That's why she never would talk about it." Candy looked out the sliding glass door with her hands on her hips. "She was so freakin' scared."

"I bet." I went around and picked up the dirty sheets and stuffed them into the empty pillowcases.

"So." Candy turned around. "Were you saying something?"

I threw the sack of linens by the door. "Yeah, am I done?"

For once Candy's hard face had a softness to it. "Not quite." She handed me the window cleaner and paper towels. "I'll go do the bathroom."

I squirted the glass and watched tiny blue rivers run to the bottom of the sliding glass door.

Candy's voice echoed from the bathroom. "The whole time she was in labor, you know what she screamed?"

I shook my head and wiped, hoping she wouldn't tell me.

"She screamed, 'Don't leave me!' Over and over, 'Don't leave me!'"

I shut my eyes, not wanting to see Mom's panicked face, but there it was, reflected in the glass. Hollow eyes, matted hair, dry, unspeaking lips.

"Claude?"

I squirted again and wiped at the face. I wiped and wiped, over and over. Five wipes and one squirt, five wipes and one squirt.

"Claude!" The voice was closer, and I turned. Candy was leaning against the bathroom doorframe.

"Yeah," I said.

"You're gonna rub a hole in that glass."

I looked at the place where Mom had been and wished she was back.

"Anyway, that's why I can't believe she's off at rehab. She ain't the type to do something like this alone. Not without telling me."

"You said that already."

I looked outside the sliding glass door at a couple on the lower deck. They had their bags packed and were ready to go. The man was dressed in lime green golf shorts and had a pink shirt on. The woman was in pink shorts and a lime green shirt, her shoulder bag hung neatly at her hip. He placed his hand on her bottom, and she smiled up at him. I watched them for another second, grateful for their absurdity, hoping they wouldn't move.

"Don't you think it's more like her to go off with Gary? Even though she didn't tell me?" I turned at the sound of Candy's voice. She was rapping the toilet brush against the doorframe and looking like she wanted a cigarette.

I put the bottle down on the table with a smack. "Stop it! Why is it so fucking hard to believe that she finally got it together? Why, Candy? Mom and I tried so hard, so many times. I told you before. This time she made a commitment to get sober for good. For real." I smacked the bottle down again. "Jeezus! What's wrong with everyone?" I whirled around and picked up the wet paper towels off the floor and threw them on the cart.

"Well, let's see, Claudine," Candy said calmly. "How many times has she gotten it together and then fallen off the wagon? Hmm?" She bent over and jiggled the brush around in the toilet. Popping her head back in the doorway, she said, "I ain't wicked smart, but I do know that your mother is kind of needy. She don't do anything alone." She turned back and flushed. Above the gurgle, I heard her mumble, "And I don't believe it cuz it ain't true."

Later, Candy followed me out to the car. She handed me my payment for the hours and held the door while I got in. Shifting from one foot to another, she reminded me of one of the rowboats tied up to the dock, rocking with the tide.

I started the motor and put the car in gear. Still, she held the door. "What makes you think your mom's at rehab?"

"Because it's true."

"Come on, Claude, don't you think we ought to contact Gary just to be sure? Or, I hate to suggest it, but should we call the police?"

"No! She's at rehab, Candy. I should know. I put her there." I pulled the door shut and backed out, leaving her shaking her head.

Candy and Linwood didn't believe me. But that's how it is with alcoholics. They alienate people all the time, and Mom had alienated her best friends and left for rehab without telling them. I guess they didn't like being out of the loop.

The unaddressed letter to Mom lay on the passenger seat. I went past the turnoff to Sea Spray Acres and drove to the post office. I pulled alongside the mailbox, addressed the letter to Serena Carbonneau, Jackson Heights, Portland, Maine, and popped it in the chute. Why did I wait so long to write her? The poor thing was probably wondering why I'd abandoned her. She'd get it in two days. I would write her every day from now on to make up for my neglect.

My shaky legs quieted as I walked into the fresh-smelling kitchen. I hung up my coat, left my shoes on the mat, and checked the messages. There was one from Candy, apologizing if she upset me and offering me a job until Mom came home.

I went to the chart. I probably wouldn't sleep. There were things that had to be finished tonight, and then I had the application to do. All-nighter tonight.

The first thing on the list was to go over the schedule to see if I was forgetting anything. I'd learned my lesson with Moonpie's mistake. I hadn't caught up with the laundry or the dusting. Even though the place looked great, I knew it would be a mistake to skip anything on the list because they'd just catch up with me later. Still, I found myself at the sink, washing my hands, wiping down the counter after I got suds on it, pushing in the chairs, doing things that weren't on the list.

I went back to the cupboard doors with Saturday and Sunday on them and read down the list until I got to the last item: dusting. Dusting could wait until Sunday, and I'd do it along with the polishing. Instead, I dragged the vacuum into the living room and plugged it in. I turned on the TV, and by the time the local news came on, I was done.

I plopped on the couch and turned the sound off. Rain came in easygoing spurts, like the conversations Liz and I used to have on the phone.

Liz would say, "I forgot to tell you what Mom said to Dad last night."

After we'd laugh about it, there would be an easy silence. Then I'd say, "Did I tell you what that dub Linwood did?"

Again, we'd laugh. Pitter-patters of conversation that didn't require hard answers.

Dear Mom,

It's day 13 now, and I am so proud of you. You have a lot of doubters. Sorry, I had to tell you that. The odds are against you, if you believe in them. I don't. I believe that if you believe enough about anything, you can make it happen. You know what I mean? Like that one time when we were hungry and your check hadn't come and we had to eat popcorn for two meals. We pretended it was exactly what we wanted for supper. And at breakfast the next morning you said, "I feel like popcorn again." I agreed that it was exactly what I wanted, too. We put in a video and crunched away until the mail came. We did that more than once.

Now it's your turn to believe:

Believe you are sober, and that sober is the way every day.

Believe in the group.

Believe that you deserve this chance to recover.

Believe in me.

—Claude

The rain was like that most of Saturday night.

Around midnight I began the essay. It was about giving back to the community. My education is my past, my present, and my future. Sounds good. Therefore I blah, ba-blah, ba-blah. Sounds nice. After I graduate, a significant part of my free time will be devoted to blah, ba-blah, ba-blah.

When I finished, I didn't look it over too hard. Did I even care? I didn't know. What would I do at college? I didn't know. What did I care about? I couldn't see beyond today's list. Today's list had ten items plus add-ons.

Laundry Day	put cat out	work on essay
shower and bathroom stuff	brush teeth	bios for Springer??
feed Moonpie	return bottles and cans	clean clean clean clean clean
get dressed, put pajamas in the washer	kitty litter (get)	

14

Sunday LAUNDRY DAY

W HEN I WOKE, IT WAS NEARLY NOON, and the political round tables were wrapping up and the weatherman was the first thing on the news. Gert was gaining strength and heading for New England. I didn't pull up the shades, didn't even look outside. I still had work to do. A bowl of Swiss muesli would power me up for everything I had left. The bios still weren't done. Mr. Springer was probably right about me not turning them in. The application needed to be finished, and I needed to do the essay over, or at least add to it.

The cupboards were stocked with unprocessed organic

food. I felt strong and safe just looking at the boxes and jars lined up in straight rows. The cookie jar was filled with my homemade muesli. It had organic oats, powdered oats, raisins, dates, walnuts, flax seeds, and cinnamon. Way easier to make than granola, which had to be cooked to a crisp.

I sat at the table grinding away, studying the organic milk carton. It said the dairy farm had happy cows and that meant healthy milk. I was about to swallow another mouthful of muesli when I felt a small but definite movement on my tongue. I spit it out and looked into my bowl. Something moved between the lumps of dates and walnuts. I stirred my spoon around, revealing several pointy ends that wriggled away from the light. Scraping away more, I saw that they were all tail. Worms. Maggots. How many bites had I taken? Bitterness filled my throat and I gagged it all onto the table, over my bowl and splattering the application envelope. How many bites? Why didn't I count? I gagged again. I should have counted.

In the bathroom I brushed my teeth and wondered what Liz would say if I told her. She'd say: There's a reason the health-food stores keep nuts in the refrigerator. There's a reason companies process foods.

I spent the afternoon sprinkling food on the counter to search out maggots. If a bag looked good, it went into the fridge. Oats and walnuts bad, the flour good. Fruit good. By the six o'clock news, the cupboards were bare again, but the fridge was full of bags and jars.

The weatherman was very grave. Probably Tuesday.

He insisted that people get duct tape, buy flashlights and batteries. I wasn't going out. I hadn't written my letter to Mom, and the post office wasn't open anyway. No, I wasn't even going to look out the window.

Dear Mom,

It's day 14. I'm remembering being sent home from school in a snowstorm and finding the house cold and the power out. It was freezing, so I crawled in bed with you and told you princess stories. I piled blankets over us and made the princess's hidden village in the folds. The snow globe sat high up on your hip, an empty bottle on the side table was an attacking soldier from another kingdom, and your wavy hair the ogre in the valley below.

We're going to have a hurricane. If you were here, you'd be scared, but I'd keep it together for you.

—Claude

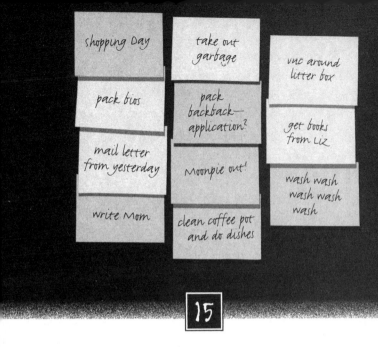

15

Monday SHOPPING DAY

AT SCHOOL IT WAS ALL I HEARD. "Gert's coming." "Batten down the hatches." "We're gonna get slammed, man!" When the bell rang for lunch, I saw Liz go the opposite direction of the cafeteria with Jenna. I headed to the library. Just as I opened the door, Ms. Frost touched my elbow.

"Claudine, we need to talk about that scholarship. You haven't done anything with it and I know a student who could use it and he'd get it into the mail by . . ."

I knew I wanted it, but I didn't even know why anymore.

There was a seed of something inside that said, *Hang on to it, Claudine. You will want it later.*

"No, I've got it—" I patted the backpack in my hand. "Well, it's not here, but it's done."

"If you're serious about this, we need to go over it before tomorrow and put it in the mail. Why don't you stay after school and we can talk a minute?"

I moved toward the library door.

Her hand was on mine. "Claudine, look at me."

I turned away, not daring to meet her eyes. They'd be full of concern.

"Claudine, let's have a meeting with Mr. Springer tomorrow morning before school."

"Why?"

"Because he's concerned, and he understands, too."

I shrugged.

"I heard about your Mom going off with a new boyfriend."

"That's just a rumor."

"Mrs. MacPhee has offered to have you until your mom gets back, or you can stay with me. Whatever you decide." She handed me a drab yellow Post-it with her number scribbled on it. "Call me. Don't lose it; it's unlisted."

"Thanks."

"And don't forget the meeting. Seven-thirty in my office, and bring the application. Deadline tomorrow."

"I've got it. No problem," I said.

I sat in the library at the window that overlooked the

field. A line of cross-country runners jogged along the field. I counted them as they disappeared into the woods.

I drove by the Community Center and saw that Liz's car was there. I couldn't go do the group thing. I couldn't see her now. Matt wasn't there anyway. I came around the breakwater and saw his car parked with the nose pointing toward the ocean. I pulled in beside him. The ocean was swelled and bursting close to the shore. The water was greener, and a warm wind blew with an undercurrent of electricity.

He stood in front of my car and banged once on the hood. I got out, and we walked to where the waves broke.

"I guess you didn't go to group either," he said.

"Not today." I let a wave soak the bottom of my pants. "Does it help? I mean did it help before?"

"Before Dad drove drunk out of his mind into a stone wall?" He worked his bare feet into the sand. "I'd told Frost I'd try it, and I didn't think I'd go more than once, but I did. And now with relatives here and the funeral and the hurricane, I just wanted to be alone." I felt his eyes on me.

I worked my feet into the sand, too, and took a look at him. His curls almost made me forget that I had a million things to do.

When I got home, I went to Mom's room and wrapped myself in her quilt and slept with Moonpie at my shoulder.

Branches thrashed the side of the trailer, and I woke up and lifted the shade. Trees and sunflowers bowed down for the arrival of Gert.

I turned on the light and brought my binder into the bed.

Dear Mom,

  Day 15 and no word from you yet.

  Every time I tell you something that I kept a secret, I feel closer to you, but with that closeness comes a dark blanket of dread. I feel it creeping toward me daily. It seeps into me while I sleep. Even now, after sleeping in your bed for half the night, I feel it.

I stopped writing and noticed my toes. The toe ring was gone. Did I lose it at the beach with Matt? I saw us digging our feet into the sand while we talked, but I couldn't remember if it had been on my toe at the time. Why did it matter anyway? It was just a toe ring.

Maybe it mattered because my mind wouldn't hold on to things the way it used to; it was operating independently, like someone else was making the decisions.

Dust/Polish Day	mail letters like you said you would	change living room around	review Saturday's & Sunday's lists
find toe ring	wash dishes	spray stain with bathroom bleach	make a long-term calendar
put cat out	get books from Liz (just do it!)	more cat food (get)	transplant wilting purple flower and look for toe ring
pack application (it's due)	move into Mom's room	do the bios for sure this time	prepare for hurricane

16

Tuesday DUST/POLISH DAY

I COULDN'T BE LATE FOR THE MEETING with Ms. Frost and Mr. Springer. I slipped the light-as-air shirt over my head and let my hair out of its clip. The new jeans that had been stiff the first few days now felt like new skin. I needed something else. I reached into Mom's bedside table for her perfume. I dabbed the scent on my wrists and neck and breathed deeply. I was transported to a pool party at Candy's last summer, when Mom fell into the pool and I jumped in and saved her. She made a big deal about it, calling me her angel and her baby girl and a gift. I don't know if she would've drowned. Probably not.

But I'd had my first flutter of suspicion that maybe Mom couldn't take care of herself after all. That maybe she was headed for a fall.

Moonpie's meow startled me. I bolted from the room to find him pawing the door. He cowered as I came toward him. That only made me want to scare him more, but I yanked open the door instead. A steady, insistent wind blew off the ocean and whistled through the metal roof. I ran outside and up the stairs to the deck. Between the big cottages, I could see the surf kicking up in front of the seawall, and cars parked alongside. Yellow slickers dotted the wall where people sat, hoping for a spray. The rain was a steady patter of fat, cold drops.

Inside, I checked over the Post-its: I had to remember the application and to let Moonpie out. I had to do those things. But I also hadn't finished the chores from the three days before.

Maybe I could stay home and hang out in Mom's room. I felt closer to her in there. Anyway, other people would skip on a day like this. Liz would stay home. Her parents wouldn't let her out of the house, I knew that for sure. But the hurricane wasn't here yet; it was just a bad storm. I checked off what was done, brushed my teeth, and decided to skip feeding Moonpie. I swished and checked my brushing job in the mirror. My heart thudded in my chest.

"Mom?"

She smiled back at me, but something was different. Something wasn't right.

"What is it, Mom?"

Her blue eyes grew dark and her skin paled. Her lips parted as she shook her head.

"Talk to me, Mom."

"Walk away," she said. "Just walk away, Claudine."

I backed out of the bathroom, ran to the kitchen, and grabbed my backpack. The car keys weren't where I'd put them, and I didn't want to be late for the meeting with Ms. Frost and Mr. Springer. Why hadn't I put THAT on the chart? It took exactly fifteen minutes to get to school, and I hadn't computed extra time for the storm. How could I have lost them? I lifted the backpack and heard the keys jingle. I flew down the steps and tripped over Moonpie, who was crouched on the middle step, squinting up at me through the rain. For a second I didn't know what to do with my muddy hands and knees. I checked my watch. If I didn't leave now, I'd be too late for the meeting. But if I didn't wash, I knew I'd never make it through the day.

Inside and under a hot spray, I watched the dirt run down my legs, through the silver anklet and between my toes, where Mom's silver toe ring shined. The toe ring. I looked around as if the shampoo and conditioner would tell me how I had found it. I looked back at the water running clean around my feet and turned it off. I put the mud-stained jeans back on, prepared for the skin-crawling sensation.

One thing I knew was that if something was bugging me, I could substitute it with another thing. On the way to school I focused on other things—the drive, counting telephone poles along the way. *One, two, three, four, five. One, two, three, four, five.*

I arrived late, ten minutes before first bell. Ms. Frost and Mr. Springer just stared at me. "I'm sorry," I said.

"Your clothes," he said.

"I fell down," I said, wishing I'd washed the pants. As soon as I said it, I felt my skin crawl with germs. Soil, especially wet soil, is teeming with bacteria.

"We're closing at noon to get the gym ready for anyone who needs to stay here," Ms. Frost said.

I dug into my backpack and took out the application envelope. "Here," I said. "And thanks." I got up to go.

She brightened. "Wait," she said, pulling out the pages.

"Maybe we ought to reschedule this," Mr. Springer said, looking at the clock.

Ms. Frost nodded. "Okay, right after dismissal. Be right here."

No, I thought. "Okay," I said.

"Gert may pass, but to be safe, are you staying with the MacPhees? You can also stay here with me at school and help with emergency management. Mostly ladling soup."

"I haven't decided."

"Just check in before you go."

Mr. Springer jiggled the change in his pockets, studying me, brows in one uneven line. He glanced over at Ms. Frost.

"I have some concerns," he said.

"You're not my parents," I said. I left the room and walked down the hall, out the door, and to the car.

I drove along the shore and turned into Deep Cove Downs, where the MacPhees lived. The roads were shiny with the cold rain that had blown into Deep Cove. The MacPhees' house and yard were the prettiest of them all, with fall decorations that achieved the perfect balance of autumn cheer and nonchalance, even in the face of Gert's wet wind.

I pulled over, debating whether to get out or not. The windows were lit up with a warm yellow glow, and a thin stream of smoke meandered from the center chimney. Two blue cars were parked in front of the garage—her mother's Saab and her dad's Grand Cherokee. I watched as Liz passed by the living room window carrying a bowl of something. Her father pretended to grab it, and they played at dodging each other.

I'd always liked being at the MacPhee house when they were like this. They made everything special, even storms. A sleepover wasn't just sleeping over, it was an event, with pizza, videos, and pretty sleeping bags. Mrs. MacPhee even bought me my own Little Mermaid sleeping bag. She'd told me that Mom's sleeping bag, the one I'd brought with me, had been accidentally taken out in the trash. From then on, my sleeping bag and nightgown stayed right there, where they were washed and folded until the next sleepover.

I think I knew what was going on, since everything I owned stunk like the trailer, like Mom. People didn't have to use words; I knew I smelled when they held their noses and moved away from me on the bus.

My heart ached as I looked into the house. I could have that again. If I asked, they'd let me stay over during the hurricane, but something kept me from getting out of the car. I was seventeen, not ten, and I didn't need Marty MacPhee providing me with fresh-smelling clothes, or Liz counseling me.

A gust of wind picked up a pile of wet leaves and swirled it into a loose tornado. I drove to the beach and parked by the seawall instead of heading right home. The ocean and the sky were the same color of moody gray, and the wind slapped the rain against the car. I rocked inside, watching the windshield blur with rain, and mentally finished the letter to Mom.

I can't believe we're not going through this hurricane together.

I put my wrist to my nose and closed my eyes as the musky perfume took me to her. I let myself remember the garden as she had expanded it last summer. A combination of a high tide and spring storm had washed in an assortment of knobby wood, smashed wooden lobster traps, and sections of an old skiff. We'd spent days hauling driftwood home in the back of the car to make raised beds.

The weekend we built those raised beds was amazing, Mom. I was in awe of you. I thought everything was going to be all right. It looked like everything was okay. We were so tired and so happy. Every so often I stared at you just because you were so into it. It was a surprise to me to see you so into something that wasn't a guy or a party or a meltdown. And the change in you? It was the one time you had stopped drinking on your own.

I wish I'd told you how proud I was.

A wave broke over the seawall and sprayed the car. I turned the key and drove toward home. Inside the trailer, the lights blinked. The fridge groaned back on, the baseboards ticked, and the answering machine flashed red and spoke to me.

"Answering machine is on. You have one message. Eleven thirty-five." After the long beep came a breathy sound, maybe a whisper, and then a click. "Mom?" I said. There was another soft click.

Outside there was another sound, a whirring sound above the rain. The wind had suddenly picked up speed.

I put my lips close to the speaker. "Is that you? Mom, it's me," I said. "Why won't you answer me?!"

The power blinked off and on, and the machine clicked again. "Answering machine is on. You have no messages."

Just walk away. Walk away and pretend you're not hurt, Claudine.

I sat down on the couch and turned on the TV just in time to see a picture of a monster hurricane over southern Maine. We were just to its north.

A sharp crack sounded above me as a limb hit the roof. A ceiling tile fell, and powdery beads scattered on the living room floor. I moved toward the closet for the vacuum but stopped short of it when the phone rang.

"How are you doing over there, dear?" Mrs. MacPhee said. "You know that Ms. Frost and I talked about having you stay with one of us, don't you?"

"Hi, Mrs. MacPhee," I said. "Yes, I know."

"Well, I'm sending Tom over to get you right now."

"No, no, I decided to stay with Ms. Frost. I'm on my way out right now."

"Oh?"

"Yeah, I was just leaving when you called."

"Oh, good. Well, I feel better then. I understand you and Liz had words. She wants to talk to you."

"I—"

"She just has your best interests in mind, Claudine."

I didn't really feel like talking, but I stayed on the line.

"Hey, Claude, you're coming over, aren't you? We need to talk."

"Talk? I don't think so. You pretty much said I was crazy."

"I didn't say that. I said you need to talk to someone. Why is it—"

"I'm helping Ms. Frost, you know, giving back to the community."

"I can't hear you very well," she said. "Claude?"

The phone line went dead. I turned on the TV. Dead. Lights, dead.

Outside, Moonpie meowed. I looked at the mess in the living room. I wanted to suck it up with the vacuum and make it clean again. I took out the broom instead and brushed it into an unsatisfying pile. The beads popped and flew over the rug, too light to stay put. I caught sight of my knees and wished I'd done a wash after school, and my hands were grimy from touching my pants.

When I had them all soaped up and the hot water running full tilt, I realized that it would run out. The water was on an electrical pump system, and now I didn't have power. *How many flushes? How many times can I wash my hands? I have to be able to wash my hands.*

I lifted the shade and looked out. The sky was an eerie green, and rain poured from it. Moonpie cried, but when I opened the door, he wouldn't come to me. I pulled it closed and latched it. I paced and thought about Liz. Why didn't I tell her to take care of her own problems? Tell her to change what she could change—herself?

There was a pop as a branch smashed in the bottom half of the kitchen window. The glass clinked into the sink, and a cold rain blew the ceiling tile beads across the rug again. I stuffed a couch cushion into the broken window and swept the beads into a corner.

Moonpie's cry was coming from somewhere behind the steps. It made me crazy. I undid the latch, and the door was sucked from my hands and slammed against the trailer.

"Moonpie, here, kitty-kitty," I called. My voice was carried off into the wind. "Moonpie, here, boy." He stopped crying when he heard me, but he wouldn't come. He crouched among the buckets and blocks of wood, old toys, and discarded tools. I crawled toward him and he moved farther away, rubbing against some wood and then setting on his haunches just out of my reach. "You'll just have to stay there, cat."

I stepped back through the doorway. Before me was a rainbow tornado of Post-its. They swirled in a crazy dance around the kitchen and living room. The cushion had fallen out of the kitchen window and a cross-draft had been created when I opened the door. The Post-its had peeled off the cupboards and walls and countertops, and now they flew toward me from all directions. It was like being in the world's biggest vacuum.

I pulled the door shut behind me, and the colored squares fluttered down around me like one giant to-do list.

For a moment I stood and stared at my Post-its. The only sound was the whining wind outside. *Just breathe and think. Think. Don't panic*, I told myself. *The daily jobs only represent seventy or eighty Post-its.* Then I remembered all the extras I'd made, thinking it was a good idea to get ahead. I swallowed a stone in my throat and sat down on the floor in the middle of the bright fluorescent squares and surveyed the damage. Every surface was covered, and each had a task written in my perfect lettering. *It's just work. It's doable. You can do messes, Claudine. You clean up very well. Take it one Post-it at a time, Claude, one Post-it at a time.*

I got on all fours to pick them up, collecting the yellows first. Some were jobs I'd already done. *Wipe the insides of the utensil drawers.* Why hadn't I thrown that Post-it away after I'd done the job? Why was I so smart in retrospect? I put the pile on the counter and felt the rush of wet wind smack me in the back.

It was Linwood. "What the hell? Serena?"

I crouched back down and began on the pink ones.

"What the—" he said, staring down at me openmouthed.

He shook his head. Pink, blue, and green squares swirled about us.

"Shut the damned door, Linwood!"

He stepped around the counter and looked at me. Again he shook his head and walked off toward the bedroom, his weather radio scratching out the NOAA broadcast: "Winds seventy-five miles per hour, the eye of Hurricane Gert bearing down on Deep Cove."

"We should get a break in a while. The eye's almost here," he said from down the hall. "Whole damned town's a disaster area. The seawall's in the middle of the road, and it ain't even high tide yet. You might even get some water back here."

I leaned against the cupboards and wrapped my arms around my knees to stop the chill that grew in my body.

I heard Linwood in the living room. "I thought you was Serena sittin' there in that mess. I guess it's a good thing she ain't here. You know how she can't stand a storm." I scanned the kitchen floor, my eyes resting on a drab yellow note. I scrambled to it and put it in the yellow pile, but it didn't match the fluorescent stack. It was Ms. Frost's telephone number. I put it in my pocket and sat back down.

I looked at my fistful of Post-its. It was a stack of multicolored squares. What a mess. My teeth chattered. "Damn you, Linwood. I lost my place."

He ignored my comment as he came into the kitchen. "Hey, you seen my flashlight? I'm helpin' down at the Seaside. It's a mess." He reached into the junk basket, and the stack of yellows scattered to the floor.

"Shit!" I said.

"Crissakes, Claude. It's no big deal." He scooped them up and set them back on the counter. "All cleaned up, see?"

Oh my god. I can do this, I thought. *I'll just do it square by square.*

"You really need dry clothes and a blanket, girl." He opened the hall door, and a tower of stuffed garbage bags fell to the floor. Kicking a bag out of the way, he said, "Holy shit. What's all this?"

"No," I whispered.

He tore open a bag. "Jeezus. What a friggin' mess!"

I covered my face. "No."

He pulled out a sweater and threw it at me. "How'd you get so wet anyway?"

The scent of Mom's cigarettes rose from it, and my throat tightened. "Moonpie's out there."

He caught sight of the silver around my ankle. "And why you wearin' that? I gave that to your mother."

I shrugged. "And she gave it to me."

He swallowed and then adjusted his hat. "Right." He took a flashlight out of a drawer and shined it on me. "You need to put on a sweater or get under a blanket." He opened the door, stirring up the colored squares again. "I'm getting my saw out of the shop, and then I'm going to help Candy. You sit tight."

When he shut the door, I watched the Post-its settle to the floor, but I didn't move to collect them. Instead I thought of the three plastic bags. Everything Mom owned was in those garbage bags. I knew that, and I wanted to open them and inhale the scent of cigarettes and vanilla musk.

Moonpie howled under the trailer. I tried to focus on the stack of Post-its in my hand, sorting them by color. I stood up and surveyed the room. It was a multicolored world of things to do, but I didn't move to fix it. Instead I sat beside a bag of Mom's things. I pulled out a blue mohair sweater and held it to my face. Mom. With shaky hands I pulled it over my head, and with it came the memory of her wearing it with her favorite black jeans. I could see her long fingers holding a cigarette, hear her laugh rising above all the others at a party, feel her dark, wavy hair touching my face. My mother gone away. I dug down into a bag and found her makeup kit. I took it to the bathroom and applied her dark brown eye shadow, mascara, and maroon lipstick. Putting on her gold hoop earrings made her appear in the mirror.

"Mom?"

"Hey, baby."

"Mom, I have to ask you something."

"Ask anything."

"Why did you start again?"

"It's simple. If I don't drink, I feel."

"What's so bad about feeling?"

"You should know."

"What are talking about?"

"You're the same as me."

"No, I'm not. I'm totally different from you. I'm the exact opposite. I'll never drink."

"You don't drink, but you cover up your feelings with too many words and with things to wash and fix. Princess, you care for everyone else but yourself."

I closed my eyes to change the pictures; they wouldn't stop coming. Too many pictures came. Mom in bed, Mom white-faced and hurt, Mom screaming at me, Mom crying, Mom begging. Me walking away.

"Angel, your Pleasure Zone is when you think everything is going according to your plans, the items all checked off your list. You think you have it under control, but you don't."

"Go back!" I picked up a jar of bath salts and smashed the mirror. The rain of glass cleared the images. The clinking of the pieces smoothed out my memory.

A muffled mew brought me back. Moonpie again. He was still under the trailer complaining. *That should teach him not to go out in hurricanes,* I thought. *Most animals can tell if a storm is brewing and they want to stay in.*

I sat on the floor beside the bags and pulled out a long Indian-print skirt and put it over my legs. I shut my eyes and let my mind play pictures on my screen.

I am emptying drawers. Mom's clothes are tumbling out and I am trying to get them all as fast as I can. I mix dirty piles with clean, and I stuff them all into black trash bags. They smell factory fresh, and I am worried that I will run out before I have finished the job. I pack her things tightly and dump whole drawers of junk into the bags. A pair of earrings are caught in her necklace, but I make myself forget it.

I stopped the pictures and took a sweater from the plastic bag and put my bare feet in it. "Mom?"

"Mmm." It was the way she'd answer when I went into her darkened bedroom.

"I'm cold."

"Snuggle in," she said, like she always did in the big bed.

I pulled out more clothes and piled them over my legs. "Tell me about when I was really little and Grandma still lived with us."

"The three of us lived together as long as we could stand it. I was seventeen, like you are, but I was a kid with a kid.

"She helped me get a routine, and it was okay for a while. Then, just as I was starting to get it, she took over. She did everything. She fed you, she put you to sleep, got you up, she cleaned everything. She even potty trained you. Nothing I did was good enough. But the last straw was one night when you had a bad dream and I went in to comfort you. You said, 'No, I want Mommy!' I told her to leave and never come back."

"Did she?"

"She left and I didn't see her for a long time. But I couldn't handle being alone, either."

A cry that I couldn't ignore rose up through the floor. I came out from under Mom's blanket of clothes and opened the door to face the wind. A slap of cold rain pelted me as I stepped down into the mud. Under the steps I could see Moonpie's eyes glow and hear him cry, but I couldn't reach him on the pile of wood where he sat. When I put my hand out to him, he went to the other side of the trailer and crouched. His eyes squinted at the wind, and his fur flattened against his shivering body. He didn't want me; he wanted Mom.

I stayed close to the sides as I made my way around the trailer to where he hid. Salty rain slapped me as I came around to the front. I reached for him, and he dodged me and scooted farther under and out the back side.

I shivered in the drenching rain. My clothes stuck to me, and water dripped from my nose and chin. The gardens were puddles of soggy herbs and flowers. The sunflowers were on the ground, their heavy heads in the puddles that had sprouted over the day. A gust of wind picked up a five-gallon bucket from across the road and tumbled it into our yard. Pushing against the steady wind, I went over and picked it up and made my way to the shop.

Inside, I waited to get adjusted to the darkness. I went to the back workbench and lit a match. Green, white, and blue sea glass was sorted into jars. Violet and silver mussel shells were piled in small, medium, and large piles. Wreath molds made from grapevine sat waiting for Mom. For what? There were chunky white candles lined up on a shelf next to a finished model. I lit one. Warm light made the blue glass glow as I turned the wreath and followed the pattern. I could see that she had created the up and down motion of the ocean, the wind, and sea life with her design.

Her plan was tacked on the wall. They were going to be candle wreaths. She'd played with some names: Sea Candles, Sea Wreaths, Sea Lights. She'd circled Sea Lights.

Clusters of glass and shells were to be glued on in an intricate design. One kind with only mussel shells, another in circles of green and blue glass, and a fancier model called for a driftwood stand.

I worked to the screaming of the wind through the old garage door. Elmer's glue was not what Mom had in mind, but I didn't have a choice. I stuck the pieces in a hurried design, racing against an invisible clock. My Sea Light was not at all like Mom's. I stared into the flame. She'd spent a lot of time in here after the summer people had gone home. When she began drinking again, I wasn't surprised. It was her usual time.

But she was making Sea Lights. So why the drinking when things were going this well? A limb smacked the roof, and I ducked. No damage, but I tipped over some candles. When I picked them up, I saw I'd uncovered a letter. It was written to Grandma:

Sept. 8
Mother,

I don't expect you to ever forgive me for being a bad daughter. I know this is a punishment. Who would hurt their kid this way? Try to understand my situation NOW. I'm in recovery. I go to a meeting when I can. My business is going well, and I hope to expand it enough so I can get off aid. I told you all this when we talked. Maybe that doesn't matter to you. But Claudine's still a kid, even though she acts like a grown-up. I didn't tell her about your letter. If she knew what you planned

*to do, she'd worry and try to fix it when she should be
thinking about her future. Please keep her in your heart
and wait until she's out of school.*

*I'm begging now, Mother. We need to stay here until
she's out of high school. Please.*

Your Daughter,

Serena

I flipped the envelope over and looked at the address.

Ruth Ann Bunker
166 Tern Sands Lane
Sarasota, FL

She'd never sent it. The back of the envelope was filled
with numbers. The cost of living here, there, food, electricity, and me. My cost. I recognized the amount of her
aid check. In the end everything was scratched out.

I tore apart the bench, looking for Grandma's letter, and
found it in the box of broken shells.

August 30

Serena,

*It was good to see you even if you didn't like seeing
me. I'm sorry things haven't worked out the way you
planned. Your flower shop idea is cute, but Gus wants to
summer in Maine and winter here. You know it's always
been my retirement plan. I'm sure we can work some-*

thing out, but you'll have to be out of there by October so the builders can at least do the foundation. It should be easy to find something with off-season rates.

    Love,
    Mother

As I tucked the letter away, a new picture of Mom formed before me. In this picture she was trying to do the right thing, tired of failing but screwing up still.

I lined up the wreaths in a straight row and blew out the candle. Her fall chores were listed on a piece of scrap wood in black marker: mulch, deadhead flowers, transplant herbs, harvest lavender, penny royal, purple statis, compost.

The rain and wind stopped like someone had turned off a faucet. The quiet made me look up. The eye of the hurricane was overhead. I took the clippers off the hook, grabbed the five-gallon bucket, and went to the garden. I started on the cosmos. They were pretty much destroyed. I picked them up and held a clump in one hand. Snip, snip, drop in the bucket. I cut more and dropped them in the bucket. I was reminded of my dream.

I'm an angel. I'm a garden angel, and I'm here to take care of things till you get back. I float from bed to bed, clipping and filling the bucket. Now purple coneflowers. They are heavy with rain and bent to the ground. Clip, snip, drop in the bucket. I finish the bed and move to another. This is an herb bed that looks tired and ready for cleaning up. I thin out the plantings. I am a garden angel.

I topped off the bucket as the wind began again. Moon-pie cried from somewhere.

"Here, kitty! Here, Moonpie!" I carried the bucket to the compost behind the workshop. I turned the corner and saw Moonpie sitting on a wet mound of dirt.

"Hey, baby, come in with me. It's starting again," I said. He acted like he didn't know me.

Rain fell in sheets again. I dumped the flower heads on the mound. Moonpie jumped back and flattened himself against the building. A moat had formed in a depression in front of the dirt pile. I stepped over it and reached for him. "Here, baby," I said. He took a step away.

I'd abandoned him. I stepped into the muck. "I won't do it again, Moonpie. I'll never leave you alone. I was wrong to forget about you." He looked at me and opened his mouth in a silent cry. I made my move. My fingers grazed his wet sides and he was gone. I was on my hands and knees in the earth. Flower heads floated around me. My hand clenched a blue tarp. I reeled back at the sight. Up on my knees now, I tucked it back down into the watery soil. Crying out at the sight of another corner, I crawled to it, praying not to see what I knew was there.

Her pale hand poked from the surface. I reached for it, cold and clean, washed by the rain.

Mom's white fingers curled, as if she were holding an invisible garden spade. A blast of white, painful light burst open the door that had been locked. No, this can't happen. Go back, go back. Lock the door. Please.

I scrambled in the muck, following the length of the

· 176 ·

tarp with my hand, pulling it up and toward me as I moved down the length of the mound, trying to cover her up and make her go away. Make her gone away to rehab. Make it so I don't know anything; make me forget.

I tugged again, and Mom's heel broke the surface and slapped in the water. It wasn't a dream. It was happening, and I was a part of it.

I took the five-gallon bucket and scooped soil into it and dumped it onto the grave. I went back and filled it again and dumped it again in another spot. The plastic guard on the handle cracked and cut into the fat of my hand. I dropped the bucket and sucked at the cut.

Why is this happening? I can't remember, so I must be crazy. If I focus, maybe I can remember. Could I have done this?

I shook out the questions and went back to the dirt pile and dropped the bucket in front of it. Bending to scoop, I ripped my gauzy shirt in the process. "Mom!" I cried, hugging the torn material to me. I filled the bucket with armfuls of composted soil and dumped it over her tarp-covered body. "Mom!" I filled another bucket and knelt in front of her, tipping it onto the mound.

I walk in after having dinner at Liz's neat-as-a-pin house, and you're there at the kitchen table, cigarette smoke fogging the place, five empty beer bottles in the middle of the table, hair all stringy like a witch. Now I get why you wouldn't come with me. You wanted to stay home and drink. It doesn't make sense. It's only the beginning of September, and besides, this time you've stopped on your own and you're doing great. Seeing you back in the drinking chair with the smoke swirling around you makes no sense to me, Mom.

The wind was dying, but the rain continued in sheets. I filled the bucket again, even though the soil was being washed away as I worked. The soggy moat that encircled her grave was almost filled in, but I still had to cover all the edges of the tarp. I grabbed the spade that leaned against the workshop. Maybe I needed to pile on some heavier soil, or maybe I knew that stepping on the spade as it penetrated the ground would trigger something more.

You throw a burning cigarette at my feet. I stomp it out and clean up the mess while you tease me for being a "neatnik." You tell me that you knew I'd clean it up. We are back to living in hell again, Mom. How dare you?

I lifted a spade full of sod and a potato-size rock and tipped them onto the grave. They tumbled down. I stabbed at the ground again and lifted. This time a round, shiny ball tipped off the end of the spade and fell at my feet. I picked it up, running my hands over the familiar surface, first wiping it on my sweater and then with the torn edge of my shirt until I could see the yellow hair and pink dress. The wooden stand had long since rotted, but my snow globe was intact. Through the smear of mud, I saw the princess stare back at me, her eyes the same intense blue as always. I ran with it to a puddle in the garden path and laid it down carefully. Cupping my hand in the water, I bathed the floating kingdom until it was clean.

It's the five beers on the kitchen table that make something in me snap. It's like you put them there to taunt me. How come you never leave a sixth beer on the table? I ask. Why is that? Is it because it would mean admitting that you've actually drunk the entire six-pack? It's no secret that you do that on a regular basis. Hiding the evidence doesn't make it untrue.

I took the snow globe back to the grave. The rain had washed off the dirt I had dumped, and a blue edge of tarp peeked out again. A taunt.

"I can't take it. I've done everything. I've tried to help you many times over, and I've finally realized something. It's not my job to fix you." You smirk at me. You're pretty far gone, I guess.

I would have had to dig all day if I wanted the tarp to stay covered. I dragged a pine bow over to the grave and covered her foot and the blue plastic that stuck out. A few more trips and I'd have it covered. The garden was a mess, full of blowdowns.

You throw your cigarette at me and laugh like it's funny. Snap. I tip over your beer. You try to save it, but you're too drunk. "Get me another and empty this, too," you say, hand-

ing me your ashtray. Instead of my usual lecture about smoking and the general nastiness of the habit, I dump it in your lap. You stare at the mess for a long time, and when you finally look up at me, you laugh. I snap again. I imagine brittle twigs breaking off one by one. I am breaking off piece by piece.

I hurl all five of your empties across the room and into the wall. One, two, three, four, five . . .

The grave was covered in sticks and twigs, but nothing was satisfactory about it. The rain continued down. Periodic gusts blew some of the lighter sticks off. I dragged over more limbs from the tree.

I reach into the fridge for number six. The one you've been hiding. I throw it like a missile. It hits the wall above your head. You are soaked. It's my turn to laugh. When you look up, you're crying like a baby. I feel bad but only for a second because I realize how good it feels to trash the place. I've been missing something. I swipe my arm across the table, just like in the movies. Papers, silverware, everything flies through the air and onto the floor. I pull out drawers and dump them onto the floor, then shake boxes of cereal and crackers onto the living room floor. The cupboard must be emptied, too. Everything. It feels so good.

You look like you might be sick, but you stand up and act all sorry, swaying and trying to hug me.

I can't believe this is you again. All over again. I bragged all over town about your fantastic recovery and how you'd done it all by yourself. I even bragged to the MacPhees.

You cry in great sobs. "I'm sorry, Angel, I'm sorry, Princess, I can't do it. I guess I can't handle bad news very well." While I pour potato chips on the rug, I am learning something. I am getting it. This is what I get, finally, after so many years of fixing you, Mom: it won't work unless you fix yourself, and if you don't, that's your problem.

I crack a chair against the counter. I'm scaring myself and I need to leave.

"Mom, you can clean up your own messes from now on."

I walk out the door without looking back. You stumble after me.

"Don't leave me, Angel! You can't leave me, Baby Princess!"

I turn and see you hanging onto the doorframe. "Don't leave me alone!" You fall, but I'm not going to help you up this time. You are drunk and begging, and it's starting all over again, but not for me. I'm not going to help you. This time you're going to get yourself out of this mess. You are going to get yourself out of this mess.

I turned over the bucket and sat in front of the grave. The rain kept falling from the sky as if the whole world were crying. It pounded away at the soil, and I watched as dots of blue tarp appeared before my eyes. I got up and ripped the pine boughs off and sat back on the bucket.

I walk to the beach and sit on the seawall. I think that maybe Liz will drive by and I'll sleep at her house. Then I realize something. I've made a decision. I was right. Not about how I

lost control, but about one thing. You do have to do the work
of recovery yourself. I was wrong about how I handled it. I
can still support you without doing it all for you—recovery,
that is. I decide not to sleep at Liz's house, and I walk home.

I apologize to you in my mind as I walk toward the trailer.
I practice saying I'm sorry. I'm ready. I'll say it out loud, too.
We'll straighten everything out. I'll help you get on your feet
again.

I heard a voice calling though the rain, making it sound
fuzzy. I peeked around the corner of the workshop and
saw Candy and Linwood going into the trailer.

I shivered and put my hands into my pockets. I felt the
folded envelope and remembered the curlicue handwrit-
ing. Mom was so young still—she even dotted her i's with
tiny circles. I missed her so much that my heart ached. I
knelt down in front of the grave and lifted the tarp.

I step into the room. The place is a mess, still. I didn't really
believe you'd clean it up, but I hoped a little. I lock the door,
ready for the deep cleaning.

"Mom?" I walk into the living room, stepping around
potato chips and crackers. "I really lost it, huh?" I kick aside
a pizza box and go into your bedroom. You're on your side
facing the wall, under the covers, and I feel little again. I
pull the shades and make it dark. This was our after-school
routine for so many days of my childhood. I sit on the edge
of the bed and look at your shape, your small waist and dark
hair. You're so much more beautiful than I am, even though

you're seventeen years older. I know that, and so does every-one else.

"Mom, let's start over. I realize some things that I didn't before I left today. I was wrong when I freaked out. I was mad, but I shouldn't have scared you like that. I was right about the recovery, though—you have to do it yourself. I'll support you, but it's up to you, and I'll do whatever I can to stay out of it. Maybe we should see someone together."

She's out of it, I think. Maybe I should save this until later.

I give you a gentle shake of the shoulder. Your body falls back on the pillow. What I think is your dark hair is really your blood. Your mouth gapes open and a thin string of spittle trails your cheek. Your half-lidded eyes look ahead at nothing.

I jump back. "No," I say. Then I lean over and jiggle your arm. It just flops.

"Mom!" I bend close and lift the mat of sticky hair. You have a three-inch slice in the back of your head. Blood has drained into the bed and covered the pillows and sheets. I'm wobbly, and the room goes from dark to pinpricks of white, but I can't faint. I have to be with you.

I lean over you and yell in your ear. "Mom! What's happening?" The odor of vomit wafts up from your lips, and I can see where it has dried your hair in stiff clumps and gone into your ear. "No, Mom, don't leave me, don't leave me now. It'll be okay. I figured it out today. We just need a bal-ance. That's what we never had, a balance. It's always one way or another. I just never figured it out until today."

I lie beside you and put your smooth hand on my cheek. "That fight was good, you know. It was the snap in my head that changed everything. That snap was good." I pull up the quilt and entwine our arms. You're cool and limp. No wiry feeling, no pointy limbs and fast moves. "I snapped and got really mad, but at the same time I realized some important things. I just learned them too late. I'm so sorry, Mom. I can fix it."

I snuggle closer and smell the musky scent of your hair mixed with cigarettes and beer. These are scents that I know, but the metallic smell of blood makes me shake.

"Mom, I'm scared." I lace our fingers together. "I never told you about another time I was scared, and I always thought I should." Moonpie hops up on the bed and sniffs your mouth. He turns a circle and lies down on your stomach.

"The time the social worker came, when I was in third grade, it was because of me." I try to relax the lump in my throat by breathing, but the smell of blood is frightening. "I couldn't get you out of bed one day. Nurse Gooch told me to call her if I was ever scared, and so I did. As soon as I told her you wouldn't get out of bed, she got so freaked out and her voice started to get loud and high and I wished I'd never called her. So I lied. I told her that you were up now, just going into the shower. I said it was a big mistake, that you were just sick, but she must have called the social worker because a lady came. I made sure the trailer was clean and you were beautiful and sober. But it was my fault that you got in trouble that day."

The night creeps in unnoticed, and I make a list in my

mind of things that I haven't told Mom. No more secrets between us. The front door rattles. It's Linwood. I look at the clock. Typical. It's ten o'clock and he wants to see Mom. I stay as still as a mouse. He swears and thumps down the steps. I hear the roar of his engine as he revs it before backing out.

I lie still and tell Mom the things on my list. About the time I buried my pee-soaked sheets and pajamas in the backyard before it was a garden. I couldn't let her see; I couldn't bear the look she'd give me. I tell her other things.

A blanket of peace wraps around me and I sleep. When I wake, I know what to do. I don't know how I've figured it all out, just that we've made this decision together, Mom and me, and I feel peaceful.

When I lift her from the bed, I hear the clink as her anklet falls to the floor, but I keep moving through the mess I made, and past the bloodstained rug by the door. I carry her, Moonpie following, through her favorite place, her garden, and lay her behind the workshop.

"Claudine!" Candy's voice traveled through the rain to me, but I stayed with Mom. I felt for her fingers and made myself small. The rain beat my back in a steady stream.

"Claudine!" Her voice was closer now, but I didn't move.

"The storm's over!" It was Linwood.

I could hear them open the shop door and call from inside.

Moonpie scrambled out of my arms and scooted around the shop.

"Mom?"

"Hey, Angel," she said.

In the dying wind, I looked around at the destruction. A spruce tree was down, pine limbs littered the garden, and water crept across the road.

"We made it, Mom."

"It's not really over. There's always the cleanup."

How deep do you dig to bury your mother?

The ground gives way to the spade. It shouldn't be this easy. I grip the handle tighter, refocus, and plunge the blade into the sweet, musty earth. The soil tumbles into the hole. Bending and scooping, I place it carefully in a pile to my right and kneel down.

How long should it be? I stretch out beside it and press the back of my head into the ground to make an indentation and dig my heels in to mark the length. I have a ways to go. I walk over to the blue tarp and grab one end. I feel the hard knobs of Mom's ankles through the blue plastic. My stomach lurches.

"It's just a heavy tarp," I say, dragging the body toward the end of the grave. I drop the legs when my palms get sweaty. "It's just a heavy tarp."

I walk backward as fast as I can until she's even with the end of the hole. Her chestnut hair peeks out from under the plastic, and I squeeze my eyes shut and mark the length with the spade.

How long? Another two and a half feet? With four neat, quick efforts, I finish the length. I dig out the inside and real-

ize that the deeper I dig, the harder it is. *Composted garden soil is easy, but below is stubborn, untended earth. I think there must be a reason they say "six feet under."*

I draw her body toward me, feel the weight of her, and wonder if I can let her go. The hole is black. It might be two feet deep, maybe less. I don't know, but I let go and she thuds to the bottom. It's an unnatural sound. I paw the earth on top of her, and I shovel until I can't shovel more. I want to be done.

I rest in the garden and look toward the beach. The moon has sunk behind the trees, and the sky over the sea is pink and purple, a hint that it is morning in Deep Cove.

"What the fuck!" Linwood and Candy stood at the corner of the shop with shining flashlights even though it wasn't dark.

"Oh my god, Claude. What are you doing out here?" Candy said.

I went back into my head and made pictures of Mom at Jackson Heights with her therapist, but it didn't work. I saw Mom in a white tractor-trailer sitting close to Gary in the front seat. I added details like music. They listened to Mom's favorite hard-rock station and ate snacks.

Candy scooched down and rested her hand on my leg. I pulled away.

"Claude? Come inside. You'll get sick."

"I can't." I took a handful of wet soil and patted it on some blue tarp that showed through. A few soggy flowers tumbled down.

"What the hell is this?" Candy said.

I looked at the muddy ground, then my dirty hands, and finally the tarp.

Linwood knelt beside me and put his head in his hands. "Oh my god." He took my arm and swung me toward him, his cap pouring off rain in streams. "What did you do?!"

I closed my eyes; I closed the door to his voice. I heard nothing.

Candy held me in a bear hug. Linwood got up and paced up and down in front of the grave like some kind of wild animal. The door in my mind opened again, wide, too wide, and a screeching light flooded my mind. I tried to hide from the noise.

It was Linwood's cry for Mom, and it blew the door wide open. His dying animal cry cut right through me, and I opened my eyes again to a blast of white pain.

feel the
feelings

look people
in the eye

say thank you
for coming

17

I MAKE A CIRCULAR HOLE with the spade and set the soil aside. The Madonna lily bulb fits snugly, and I sprinkle bonemeal the way Mr. MacPhee told me to. I place the snow globe and a letter on top of Mom's casket. It says:

Dear Mom,

Princess is not just bright blues and yellows. She is brave, courageous, intelligent, tolerant, and loving. She will protect you, Mom, and besides that, judging by Grandma's reaction when she saw it, I'm pretty sure it was yours before it was mine.

And here's the last thing I forgot to tell you. I forgot to say that I loved you all the while you were drunk and all the while you weren't. Even when I was taking care of you instead of the other way around, I loved you deep and true. If I'd known it was okay to be angry AND to love someone, it would have been better for both of us. I think of you when I'm in the garden.

—Claudine

I take a spade full of soil and sprinkle it over the letter. Behind me Candy cries and blows her nose.

We had to wait two weeks to have a service. I needed to get better, and someone had to find Grandma and tell her. I wouldn't do it. Candy found Ms. Frost's telephone number in my jeans and called her. I stayed there for a while, and sometimes Candy slept over at the trailer so I was never alone. But the hole I carry inside me makes me feel that way at times. Grandma's here now, and I still feel very alone. I'm the guest now in my trailer. It's not home anymore.

We stand in a circle around Mom's headstone. The MacPhees insisted on buying it for me and Mom. I wasn't so sure, but then nobody could find Grandma, so I said sure, she'd like that. Mom never had a problem with the MacPhee favors—it was me.

I am still and silent, but I let myself feel everything around me. Every cry from Candy is a knife to my heart; even Linwood's frozen stare, a stab of pain. But along with the pain I feel other things. I feel people rub my back, squeeze my shoulder, and say things like, "Call me any-time."

And each changing leaf is so amazing since I opened my eyes. I let the autumn colors cut deep as they fall from the trees. I don't want to go back to that deep, dark place, my cave of denial. I won't hide my shame inside where it grows so big, it buries me alive. I am awake now.

We drive to Seaside Cottages, where people have brought food to share. Candy has laid out a table heaped with food and drinks. Ms. Frost and Mr. Springer sit alone, munch-ing on deviled eggs and talking. They smile a little when I come over. For a second I don't speak, I just feel. I weigh each emotion to see if it's a real feeling or a cover-up feel-ing—the kind I have so I don't have to feel the real one.

This is a real one; I know it. I'm glad to see them. I'm grateful.

"Hi," I say.

"Sit down," Mr. Springer says, patting the bench.

"I'm glad you came."

He looks at his empty plate. "We wanted to," he says.

"Claudine, we'll be here for you whenever you need us," Ms. Frost says.

I think about this. They both look like they might cry, and I let myself have a feeling about it. I can't put my fin-ger on it and I decide it feels weird, but it's okay. I say, "Thanks."

We look at one another. It's a look I've never shared with adults. I think it might be honesty, or understanding. I like it.

Over at the food table I think I see Matt. He's wearing a sweater and looks smaller than usual. I see the curls resting on his shoulders, and when he turns sideways, I know it's him. I walk over.

He touches my arm. I blush.

"I'm sorry about your mom."

"Thanks. And thanks for coming."

"Everyone's here," he says. I look around and see Hanna, Chris, Blake, Willa, and Deb. Lydia and Mrs. MacPhee are talking, and for a second I want to stop them, but why, I think, why do that? What feeling is that? I'm too tired to figure it all out, but I know I can't hide anymore.

"If you want to talk, just give me a call," Matt says.

"I will. I think I'll call you." I look right into his eyes and I don't turn away. I start to count to five but stop myself.

Instead I say, "You know the hole, the unfillable one that aches day and night?"

Matt nods and looks away. I think I may have said too much, and I wish I had counted instead.

"It helps to talk about him," Matt says. "It seems like it would be the opposite, but it hurts and then it feels better. I'm a better listener than I used to be. Really." Then he punches my arm gently.

Hard fingers squeeze my arm and pull me away from him. It's Grandma. "Let's chat, dear."

I try to recognize something in her too-tanned face. The deep lines tell me that most of her day is spent sitting in the Florida sun, not working.

"What is it, Grandma?"

"Why don't you come back to Florida with me? It'll be a fresh start."

I still don't remember her. Then she cocks her head and brushes my hair from my eyes. I remember now, but I don't feel anything good and I should, because that's what I've been trying to do.

"No, Grandma, you go ahead. I need to finish out the year here, and then maybe I'll visit."

I'm shocked to see tears in her eyes.

"What is it?" I hand her one of my soggy tissues.

"Nothing." I'm betting she's feeling some shame like the rest of us who loved Mom. Could we have done more? I wonder that every day.

"You go ahead back, then, Grandma."

"Okay. And we'll keep in touch for sure, Claudine. The trailer is yours for now. Don't worry about it." It's a guilt gift, but I'm fine with that. She kisses me and disappears into a group of people near the door. I have a feeling her stuff will be gone when I get back to the trailer.

Liz is standing with a plate of mini-quiches. I haven't talked to her since the day of the hurricane. When she calls and Candy or Ms. Frost holds the phone out to me, I freeze. I have no bearings in this new relationship where she is confident and I am the messed-up one. I don't know how to be me now.

Liz sees me watching her and comes over, holding out the plate. I take a quiche, but I don't eat it.

"Claude, something terrible happened, but you and I are okay."

I turn and start walking. Everything about her reminds me of my lies. My deep denial, the professionals call it. Liz knew I was in trouble. She knew me when I didn't know myself. So why am I angry at her?

She stops me. "Come on, we're like sisters, Claude."

I feel my throat tighten.

"I want to be there for you whenever you need me," she says.

She is so good. She's doing the right thing again and I am frozen.

"And I need you to be there for me. You know, those times when I need to talk. There's nobody who knows me like you do. You have to come back and be there for me. That's what friends do."

This penetrates my shield. She still needs me.

She sets the quiches down and puts her hands on my shoulders. "I miss you, Claude." The wisps of her silky hair brush my cheek as she grabs me up in her hug. "I can't lose you."

Hugging her back, I say, "I can't lose you. And I can't lose me either."

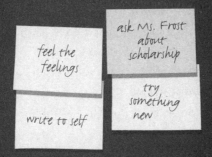

feel the
feelings

ask Ms. Frost
about
scholarship

try
something
new

write to self

18

THE SEAWALL IS BACK IN PLACE, and people are parked along the beach. Lazy waves slap at the rocks like the hurricane never happened. I sit on the hood of the car and watch them come and go. The tide is going out.

It's late October, but my feet are bare. I touch the anklet, trace the letters, and feel the coolness of the links as I unclip it. I put it to my lips and pull my arm back to heave it into the waves but stop.

I'm not ready to let Mom go, and I decide I don't have to. Clasping it around my ankle again, I think about second chances and how everyone has them. They come right after a mistake, and before making another choice, but you have to feel your feelings first.

I've been seeing a friend of Lydia's named Dr. Palmer. He's okay. He mostly listens, but every once in a while he asks me a question or says something to make me see things differently. Like last week, after I told him about messing up my chance at the Charles Hart Scholarship.

I went on and on about how I screwed up, and Ms. Frost would be mad at me, and Candy would be disappointed, and how I was just like Mom, and the MacPhees wouldn't be surprised, and all he said was, "So?"

"Well, it's true," I said.

"And?" he said.

"Well, I did mess up."

"It's okay to make mistakes, Claudine."

My throat closed and I forced myself to swallow.

"You missed that scholarship, and it's okay."

I shook my head and looked at my fingertips. They were sore, but beginning to heal with the help of Candy's hand cream.

"Think about it. What's the worst-case scenario?" he said.

"Everyone knows I didn't get it."

"So?"

"I can't afford college without it."

"Are there other scholarships?"

"I don't know," I said.

"How can you find out?"

"I can ask Ms. Frost."

"How do you feel right now?"

"Ashamed. Embarrassed. Both."

"Why?"

"I screwed up."

"Do you have any other feelings?"

I sigh loudly. I don't want to do this. He's digging again. He wants to talk about Mom. "I'm scared."

"About what?

"Talking about it."

"Talking about what?"

"Mom."

"Her death?"

I nodded my head.

"Why?"

"It'll be real if I say it out loud."

"Even if we don't talk about it, it's already real, Claudine. It really happened."

I pick up the basket and walk the beach collecting sand dollars, starfish, and sea glass to take home to the garden. I notice the new skin that grows on my fingertips and nails. New skin and new feelings.

There's so much debris left from the hurricane, but it can wait. Instead of filling the basket to the top, I set it on a rock. I feel a surge of something. I'm not sure why it is, but I feel like running. I begin with a slow jog down the beach, then I speed up a little and run in the waves. They are small, baby waves, and I run fast through them, making my lungs strain. I imagine I'm on the cross-country team. I wonder if they ever practice on the beach.

My breathing comes in fast puffs, and I smile to myself. Then I laugh as I identify the feeling.

It's hope.